"You're not going to carry me upstairs!"

Storm protested against Jago's lifting her into his arms, but her protest was in vain. It wasn't difficult for him to guess which room was hers.

"You have lovely skin," he told her softly as he dropped her gently onto her bed. His hand feathered a caress.

Shock trembled through her, and as though in a trance, she watched the slow descent of his head, his lips silky against her throat, teasing and tantalizing until she clenched her hands desperately at her sides to prevent them from sliding around him.

He had told her that she had a lot to learn. He had insisted that only he could teach her. Suddenly she realized that this was a lesson she would not forget....

PENNY JORDAN

tiger man

Harlequin Books

TORONTO • LONDON • LOS ANGELES • AMSTERDAM
SYDNEY • HAMBURG • PARIS • STOCKHOLM • ATHENS • TOKYO

Harlequin Presents edition published January 1982
ISBN 0-373-10477-4

Original hardcover edition published in 1981
by Mills & Boon Limited

CHAPTER ONE

'COME on in, Storm,' David Winters invited, when he saw the familiar female shape of his Advertising Controller hovering anxiously outside his office door.

'I've only been back a few minutes,' he added, as Storm did as she was bid, dropping a light kiss on her cheek.

'Yes, I know,' Storm agreed, too preoccupied to question the almost passionless embrace and her own lack of reaction to it. She and David had been going out together for over a year and although Storm had no doubts about her love for him she acknowledged that it did lack the passionate intensity she had heard discussed among her contemporaries. But this was how she wanted it. With David she felt safe; their relationship was as comfortable as a well worn shoe. And as boring? She dismissed the thought as disloyal and concentrated instead on the news which had brought her to his office in the first place.

David was the controller and one of the shareholders in the independent radio station, he and his team ran from the small market town of Wyechester, broadcasting throughout the Cotswolds. Still in its very early infancy, the station had been going through a bad patch lately, with audience ratings dropping and complaints from several of their backers who had looked upon the venture as a potential source of unlimited revenue. Privately Storm thought David could have done far better in his choice of co-shareholders, but she was far too loyal to him to say so.

Three weeks ago he had been summoned to London for a discussion concerning the future of the radio station, with the Independent Broadcasting Authority, and it was the results of this discussion that had brought Storm hot-foot to David's office. Passionately dedicated to the success of their venture, she asked anxiously.

'Well, how did it go? Are they going to revoke our licence?'

David shook his head.

'It's not quite as bad as that,' he assured her.

'Oh, David! You managed to persuade them to give us another chance!'

For a moment he seemed about to agree, and then he admitted unhappily:

'Not me. It was all Jago Marsh's doing.'

'Jago Marsh?' Storm stared at him. 'How did he come to be involved? I should have thought the great white wonder of the media was far too lordly to involve himself in our paltry affairs,' she said bitterly.

Jago Marsh had an unparalleled reputation in the world of independent television and radio. Storm had only seen him in the flesh once. She had been a student at the time and he had visited her college to give a lecture.

How excited she had been at the time! He had been something of a hero to her in those days. Everyone who knew anything about the media knew of his meteoric rise to fame and fortune. He had started with the B.B.C. and then progressed to various independent radio stations before starting up his own channel in London and turning it into an overnight success.

Storm had soon been disillusioned, though. Oh, his lecture had been stimulating enough, and his darkly handsome face and athletic physique had given him a presence it was hard to ignore. However, he had concluded his lecture on a note which Storm personally thought unwarranted and cheap.

Her own interest in advertising had developed while she was still at school, coupled with an enthusiasm for local radio which had led to her wholehearted belief that for the small, local business, there was no better form of advertising, and to this end she was determined to find herself the sort of job that would give free rein to her enthusiasm.

It had come rather as a dash of cold water, therefore, to hear Jago Marsh, whose career she had followed with such interest, announce in his crisply autocratic voice that by and large he considered that the field of local radio was best left to the male sex.

He had elaborated on this claim by adding that it was his experience that girls looked upon local radio as a stepping stone to a television career with all its attendant glamour.

His accusations had stung and Storm considered them grossly unfair. She had wanted to tell him as much, but the length of his lecture had left no time for questions.

Still nursing her indignation, she had seen him leaving the college. A long, sleek car was waiting for him and in it sat a perfectly groomed blonde, her voice clearly audible to Storm as she murmured seductively, 'Ah, there you are at last, darling. I thought you must have been detained by one of those wretchedly adoring little girls one always meets at these places.'

Jago Marsh's reply had been equally clear.

'They wouldn't have detained me for long. Adoration has always bored me, although most of the time I suspect that it's merely a means to an end—you can have my body if I can have a job. If I had my way women would be banned from the media entirely.'

He was despicable, Storm had seethed, watching him drive carelessly away, but from that day on she had doubled her efforts to do well at college, determined that if and when she was fortunate enough to get a job she would do it as well as—and better than—any man.

Aware of her anger, David wondered where she got her unbounded energy from. Hair the colour of sun-warmed beech leaves curled riotously round a small heart-shaped face. Eyes of a deep, misty-violet frowned determinedly behind a fringe of thick dark lashes, her small chin tilted firmly as she waited for his reply.

'It was unfortunate that he should be there.' David admitted. 'I bumped into him in the foyer. We started in the B.B.C. together. He asked me what I was doing in town.' He shrugged tiredly. 'He could have found out easily enough anyhow, so I told him, and the next thing I knew he'd taken over.'

Typical of the man, Storm thought briefly.

'I suppose I ought to be grateful to him for salvaging something. I'm sure the Authority were going to revoke our licence. Those last opinion poll results about our programmes were pretty damning. Of course Jago didn't lose any time in pointing out to me that we were badly undercapitalised.'

Privately Storm had to acknowledge that this was quite true. Apart from the small number of shares held by David the major proportion of the remainder were held by a local businessman, Sam Townley, who owned a large supermarket chain. Storm did not like Sam. She thought him both grasping and inclined to cut corners where he thought it might be to his own advantage, and he was very begrudging of the money spent on what was really basic equipment for the radio station. It had been Storm's opinion for a long time that David should seek another investor, but he had not seemed inclined to agree, and in some ways she blamed their present problems on this reluctance, although she would never have admitted it to a soul. The shortage of money had made it impossible for them to branch out in ways that might have ensured their success, but it didn't help to hear her own views reinforced by Jago Marsh.

'Does he have any suggestions as to how we might improve our capital?' Storm enquired sarcastically.

David regarded her unhappily.

'Not our capital, perhaps, but as far as our services go, he had plenty to say.'

He paused, and something in his expression communicated itself to Storm.

'There's something else, isn't there?' she asked slowly. 'Something you haven't told me.'

David had his back to her. At thirty-two he had already developed a vaguely defensive stoop, his fair hair falling untidily over his eyes, the suit he had worn for his journey to London, hanging a little loosely on his narrow frame.

'The only way the I.B.A. would agree to continue our licence was if Jago came in with us in an advisory capacity.'

For a moment Storm was too taken aback to speak, and then she rallied, exclaiming bitterly:

'And how is he supposed to do that? The last thing I heard was that he was off on a lecture tour of the States—I read it in the paper only the other week. But I suppose he's so egotistical that he thinks he can advise us, give his lecture tour and run his own station all at the same time. After all, a small venture like ours shouldn't take up more than half an hour or so of his time every other week. Is that it? I suppose we ought to be grateful,' she added before David could speak. 'At least he'll be out of our hair, but it makes me so mad. When we eventually do make a success of the station—and we will, I know we will, he'll collect all the congratulations and we'll have done all the work.'

'It's not going to be quite like that, Storm,' David told her. 'Jago isn't going to the States. He's cancelled his tour, and he says the London station is running perfectly now. He's pretty confident of the management he's got down there. He's got interests in television too, of course, but right now what he's looking for, so he told me, is a new challenge, a chance to get back to the roots of local radio and see how it's changed in the last decade. He's coming down here, Storm, to run the station himself.'

Storm had grown steadily paler as David delivered this speech. Now she stared at him in disbelief.

'He can't be!' she objected. 'Oh, David, surely you didn't agree to that!'

'I didn't have much chance,' he told her defensively. 'The I.B.A. were all for it. As far as they're concerned he can't do any wrong. He had plenty of pull with them, I could tell that right away. How could I make them listen to me? They've given us another three months to try and turn the corner and . . .'

'They?' Storm asked dangerously, her eyes flashing. 'Or Jago Marsh? What does he hope to prove by doing this?'

'It's the challenge that attracts him.' David replied a little bitterly. 'He hasn't changed since we were at the B.B.C. together, unless it's to become even more ruthless.'

'I suppose he think's he's going to trample all over us, acting the big "I am",' Storm complained. How well she remembered the cool mockery with which he had outlined his objections to women in the media, somehow subtly conveying the opinion that women had only one role in his life. Well, if he thought he was going to treat her as a sex object he had another thing coming!

'Why did you let the Authority foist him off on you?' she asked David unhappily. 'If they have to put someone in to monitor our progress, why not someone else?'

'If it had been left up to them I think they would have revoked our licence altogether,' David admitted, not willing to admit that the Authority, far from giving him the opportunity to state his reluctance to have Jago join them, had seemed to expect him to be overwhelmed with gratitude for his intervention.

'Your own job should be safe enough,' David told her. 'You're very highly qualified, Storm, and your references from Frampton's were excellent.'

'But I haven't exactly achieved great success since I've

been here, have I?' Storm said bitterly.

She had come to the job from her previous position as an accounts assistant with a large advertising agency in Oxford, full of enthusiasm and ideas, a plan of campaign carefully mapped out from judicious observation of the way in which other successful radio stations handled their advertising. But the last twelve months had not proved as promising as she had hoped.

'Time we weren't here, Storm,' David announced, glancing at his watch. 'Meet you downstairs in ten minutes?'

Storm nodded. David often gave her a lift home and it was these shared journeys which had initially given rise to their romance.

'When are you going to tell the others?' Storm asked from the door.

'They already know,' David told her tiredly. 'Pete was waiting for me when I got back, and there didn't seem any point in keeping it a secret.'

Pete Calder was one of their two D.J.s, something of a live wire, who made no bones about the fact that he found Storm attractive. An easy friendship had developed between them, and Storm sensed that Pete would have liked to take it a stage farther had she been agreeable.

It was five to six when she walked into the cluttered, boxy room that doubled as an office-cum-staff room-cum-canteen, to collect her coat and bag. Four people were lounging round a table drinking mugs of coffee and munching broken biscuits; the two technicians who worked on the evening shift—Radio Wyechester operated twenty-four hours a day—the disc jockey for that evening, who was Pete, and one of the typists, a small fair-haired girl named Sue Barker.

The buzz of gossip faded a little when Storm walked in. Pete beckoned her over, brandishing his cup.

'Got time for one before you go, my lovely?' he asked

Storm. 'Or is the great man waiting?'

Storm's eyes sparkled a little at this sarcastic reference to David, but wisely she let it go. It wasn't possible to keep their personal relationship private in such a compact group and sometimes Storm bitterly resented Pete's contention that because David was quiet and introverted, he must also be weak and spineless. She loved David's gentleness, she often told herself, and if at times he seemed to bow down to others, it was because he was innately too considerate to argue. Personally she could not think of anything worse than the type of man who dominated with his personality.

'I've got a few minutes yet,' she told Pete, guessing from his excited air what had been the topic of conversation before she walked in.

'What do you think about Jago Marsh joining us?' Pete asked confirming her thoughts.

He had deep blue eyes and wildly curling fair hair. Under his air of casual bonhomie lurked a keen brain and an acid sense of humour, but Storm refused to let him get under her guard, and a certain sense of mutual respect had grown up between them. Pete was the more popular of their two D.J.s, and at twenty-three a year older than Storm.

She was too angry for caution and answered furiously, 'That the I.B.A. have a nerve off loading him on us!'

'Come on, Storm,' Pete objected. 'We ought to be down on our knees thanking God that we've got him. Face it, David might be a nice guy, but there was no way he was going to make this station work. With Jago Marsh in charge . . .'

'In charge! He's coming in in an advisory capacity, that's all,' Storm reminded him. 'David's still in charge.'

For a moment there was silence from the others, and then Pete's eyes crinkled in amusement.

'That's our Storm! Faithful to old David until the last.

Jago's going to have to watch himself with you around, honey!'

General laughter greeted this sally, and Pete slipped a friendly arm round Storm's shoulders, pulling her against him.

'Don't go into a sulk on me,' he teased. 'Even you can't deny that our David isn't exactly the dynamic type. He's a nice guy, Storm—no one denies that—but you've only got to look at our ratings—at the way he refuses to stand up to Sam Townley and tell him outright that we won't get anywhere until we get some decent equipment, to see that he just isn't cut out for this game. You need to be tough!'

'Like Jago Marsh, I suppose you mean?' Storm interrupted bitterly.

'Be fair!' Pete objected. 'You've only got to look at our ratings to see how badly we're doing. No one knows that better than you.' Pete was ambitious and his eyes were hard as he looked at her mutinous face. 'Come on, Storm, you can't have forgotten what happened when you went to see old man Harmer already.'

Storm had not! John Harmer's comments had rankled and she was still smarting from her interview with him. Harmer Brothers were the largest local employers. They owned two woollen mills, turning out fine cloth in a small and exclusive range of tweeds, using Cotswold wool. Storm had spent weeks preparing an advertising campaign to put before Mr Harmer, but she had got scant response. Despite the rates she had offered—pared down to the bone—and the fact that she had pointed out their widespread audience and limitless possibilities, John Harmer's reception had been the opposite of enthusiastic.

'Waste money advertising on a two-bit outfit that only appeals to kids and housewives?' he had scoffed. 'I'm a businessman, my dear, not a philanthropist.'

His words had stung and continued to do so, because

his comments held an element of truth. Many, many times Storm had tried to persuade David to adopt a more forward-thinking attitude; to develop their range so that they could include more topical subjects; to promote a weekly disco as the other, more successful stations did, but all her suggestions had been met with a gentle but definite rebuff. However, she chose not to remember her past disappointments now, concentrating fiercely instead on her loyalty to David, ignoring the small voice inside her asking if their 'adviser' had been anyone but Jago Marsh she would have reacted more favourably.

She despised the man, she told herself angrily, taking no part in the excited conversation going on around her as the others discussed the changes likely to be made.

'I can tell you one thing,' Pete announced confidently. 'He won't put up with Sam Townley's tricks for very long. I mean, just look at this place for a start . . .'

Their studios were shabby and ill-equipped, Storm was forced to admit.

Initially it had been David's intention to house the venture in purpose-built offices just outside Wyechester, but Sam Townley had soon put a stop to such ambitious thoughts. As the main investor he claimed that he should have the greatest say in how their capital was spent, and David found himself forced to take up a tenancy of some cramped offices over one of Sam's supermarkets.

'What do you think Jago Marsh is going to do?' Storm asked Pete angrily, infuriated by his contemptuous dismissal of all that David had tried to do. 'Wave a magic wand and produce a modern, fully equipped radio station?'

'Well, whatever he does it can't be worse than David's efforts.' Pete fought back. 'For God's sake, Storm! You might be in love with the guy, but when are you going to see him as he really is? You feel sorry for him because he's always the under-dog, but whose fault is that? I don't know what you see in him . . .'

They had had this argument before, and as always it put Storm on the defensive. She could not explain to Pete, with all his frank appreciation of the modern approach towards sex, that with David she did not feel threatened, forced to give more of herself than she wished, either emotionally or physically, and that she loved him for his gentle acceptance of this.

As she got up to leave she was frowning unhappily. Just what did they think Jago Marsh was? A magician? Well, they would soon be disillusioned. He was a cold, ruthless man, incapable of understanding the feelings of others, arrogant and overbearing. Without the slightest effort she could remember every line of his hard-boned face, every inflection of his voice as he denounced her sex, and she was almost trembling with anger as she stepped out into the street to meet David.

He was sitting in his car waiting for her, and Storm smiled at him as he opened the passenger door of the homely little Ford. He made no attempt to kiss or touch her despite the fact that the car-park was deserted and he had been away from her all day.

It was just over half an hour's drive to the village where she lived with her parents, and they normally sat in a companionable silence listening to Radio Wyechester.

Storm's father was a lecturer at the local university and Storm had grown up in the Cotswolds and loved them very dearly.

It was October, one of Storm's favourite months. Summer had lingered on this year, and the trees were just beginning to turn, the harvested fields a bright, lush green where the new growth showed through. Opening her window, Storm relaxed in her seat, enjoying the fresh air. It was colder today, with a sharp little breeze that heralded the end of their Indian Summer. She shivered suddenly with a presentiment that the wind of change was blowing into their lives in more ways than one. Jago Marsh! Why did it have to be him of all people?

'Something wrong, Storm?' David asked gently.

'It's just this business of Jago Marsh,' she admitted uneasily. 'I can't help wishing you'd never met him . . .'

'You'll be more than a match for him,' David assured her. 'He isn't used to women standing up to him.'

'No, I suppose they're more likely to fall prone at his feet,' Storm retorted caustically.

'Or on his bed,' David said very dryly.

So she hadn't been mistaken in her impression that Jago Marsh was a man who considered women were put on earth to serve only one purpose, Storm reflected wrathfully, turning up the volume of the radio as a news broadcast finished.

The next programme was a current affairs discussion, hosted by Mike Varnom, their other D.J.. It was a relatively new departure for them and Storm was anxious to hear how it went.

The subject under discussion was the Common Market and the problems of exporting English lamb to France. The discussion, involving a couple of local farmers and their Euro M.P., should have been interesting, but somehow the speakers lacked conviction. Mike was constantly deferring to the politician, and Storm's brow creased as she listened to the broadcast, the lovely countryside through which they were driving forgotten.

'Oh no, Mike!' she protested in dismay at one point, when he cut right across one of the farmer's angry arguments.

'The discussion *was* getting pretty heated, Storm,' David pointed out mildly when she turned to him.

'But that's the whole point,' she objected. 'Involvement—that's what we're all about.'

David laughed.

'Such a fierce little thing! I suppose if you were conducting the interview you'd be making mincemeat out of our Euro friend?'

'Well, we are talking about the farmers' livelihood. You know how high feeling is running locally against the Common Market subsidies.'

'Umm—well, nothing can be achieved by attacking him broadside on, Storm. He isn't a free agent, you know. Governments dictate policy . . .'

'And governments are made up of men and women—like you or me. If we make our protests loud enough and long enough . . .' she sighed in fond exasperation when David shook his head.

'I'm not going to argue with you,' he told her mildly. 'Sit back and enjoy the scenery. I refuse to have my journey home ruined by a discussion on politics. I've got enough of that to contend with during the day.'

Storm was instantly remorseful, remembering his discussions with the Authority, but the ineffectualness of the programme lingered on, niggling, when she tried to relax her mind into other channels.

'Shall I see you tonight?' she asked David casually.

He shook his head.

''Fraid not. I've got to get some work done if I'm going to be ready to face the sort of inquisition Jago will have in mind. Why don't you go out with Pete and that crowd?' he asked her.

That was another good thing about David, Storm reflected. He wasn't at all possessive. In a mature, well-balanced relationship there should be no need for jealousy.

The duck-egg blue sky was turning primrose when David stopped the car at the end of her parents' drive. Leaning across her to open the door, he kissed her lightly.

Storm's mother was in the garden. A placid, plump woman in her late fifties, she often found it difficult to understand how she had managed to produce such a turbulent firebrand.

Storm was the youngest of the family and the only girl. Both her brothers had left home several years earlier. John, the elder, was a mining engineer who lived and worked in Australia, making very infrequent trips home. Ian, three years older than Storm, was an oil technician who spent half his life commuting between various far-flung outposts of the world, looking for oil, and consequently he too was a rare visitor to the sprawling old house, nestling against the protective lee of the Cotswolds.

'I thought I ought to cut the last of the roses before the frost gets them,' Mrs Templeton said to Storm. 'It makes the garden look so bare, though,' she added, looking regretfully at her denuded bushes. 'David drop you off?'

'Mm. Let me carry those for you,' Storm offered, relieving her mother of her secateurs and gloves. Although her parents were quite fond of David, Storm sensed that they did not entirely favour her relationship with him. They were such a pair of romantics, she thought affectionately, no doubt they would have preferred her to fall fathoms deep in love. Her mind shied away from the prospect, apprehension shivering through her, as she admitted that she was frightened of the commitment such a relationship would entail. Deep waters were not for her, she decided firmly as she followed her mother into the house.

'Dinner won't be long,' Mrs Templeton warned as Storm headed for the stairs.

'I'll just have a quick shower, then,' Storm replied.

Because of the amount of equipment crammed into their inadequate premises it was always uncomfortably warm in the studios and Storm liked to refresh herself with a shower before sitting down for her evening meal.

What would Jago Marsh make of their premises? she wondered, a sardonic smile touching her lips as she prepared for dinner. The offices themselves were bad enough, but worse by far was their outdated and hopelessly inefficient equipment. Their outside broadcast van had barely passed its M.O.T., in fact Pete had sworn that it was purely on account of Storm's pleading violet eyes that it had scraped through at all, and so it was with all their gear. Mikes failed to operate, turntables refused to turn; splicers tangled the tapes, and it was always the exhausted staff who had to work on painstakingly righting the faults caused by unreliable equipment. Storm's lip curled as she thought of Jago Marsh sitting up nursing a faulty transmitter. Well, he was in for a few shocks if he expected his existence to be cushioned with velvet once he joined Radio Wyechester, she thought with grim satisfaction.

Her parents were already seated when she entered the dining room. Storm's father was a lecturer at the local university, a tall, still handsome man in his late fifties, with a pronounced sense of humour, and a comprehensive understanding of the young.

Although there were only the three of them left at home, Mrs Templeton insisted on a certain degree of formality for their evening meal, and although breakfast was normally a rushed affair with Storm swallowing a quick cup of coffee, standing up in the kitchen, and Mr Templeton munching toast, hidden behind his newspaper, dinner was always a leisurely meal, eaten with due regard for the digestion.

Her mother was an excellent cook, and since Storm had no need to worry about her weight, she tucked into her steak and kidney pie with every evidence of enjoyment.

Richard Templeton lectured in economics and had the dissecting mind of the intellectual. The Templeton household had never suffered from a lack of stimulating conversation, and the dinner table had been a favourite platform for the younger generation to launch its attacks on the elder throughout the boys' and Storm's adolescence. Nowadays there were no longer heated discussions about pop singers and curfews, nevertheless Storm enjoyed pitting her wits against her father's razor-sharp mind—Templeton Père had the disquieting knack of sniffing out the weaker points of an argument, although what she lost in logic Storm more than made up for in vehemence.

'Had a good day, Storm?' Mrs Templeton enquired when she had served the apple pie. Storm had been somewhat subdued during the meal, and it struck her that she was looking far from happy.

'Not really,' Storm admitted. Her parents knew all about the problems suffered by the station, and both waited sympathetically to hear her news.

'We're being allowed to keep our licence,' she told them, 'but with certain provisos—one of which is Jago Marsh.'

'*The* Jago Marsh?' her father enquired with some interest. 'Well, I don't know why that should make you look so miserable. If you ask me he's just what your outfit needs. Incredible, the progress he's made during the last few years. There can't be many people more experienced in the media today, and I'm sure he'll be able to do a damned sight more for you than David's ineffectual . . .' He broke off as his wife kicked him warningly under the table.

'I'm sorry, Storm,' he apologised, 'but although I like David, I don't think he's cut out for such a competitive business. I never have done . . .'

'But you admire a man like Jago Marsh,' Storm said bitterly, 'a man who constantly features in the gossip columns—changes his girl-friends like other men change their shirts, is known to be completely ruthless and. . . .'

'Most reprehensible,' her father agreed, surveying her flushed cheeks with twinkling eyes. 'What is it that you object to most, Storm? That he's been appointed to try and make some order out of David's chaos, or his romantic proclivities?'

'I object to everything about him,' Storm retorted, abandoning her attempts to reason logically. 'You don't know him like I do. He's the original male chauvinist pig!'

Mr Templeton raised an eyebrow 'You know him?'

'Oh, you know what I mean,' Storm said crossly. 'I've read about him. I've heard him lecture, I've actually seen him say that women have no place in radio . . .'

'Scarcely the basis on which to claim a knowledge of the man,' her father pointed out. 'Look, Storm, I can understand how you feel, in some ways, but I think you're deliberately blinding yourself to the truth. Just because you personally don't like the Jago Marsh you've created in your imagination it doesn't mean that he won't do a good job. How often have you come home bemoaning the fact that David has squashed one of your ideas?'

It was true.

'That's different,' she protested.

'Because you're the one to do the criticising? Not good enough, my girl, that's not logical. Not good enough at all. As it happens I've heard Jago Marsh lecture too, and I got the impression of a man who knows where he's going and when. Granted he won't suffer fools gladly, but then why should he?

'If you two are going to engage in one of your arguments I'm off to the kitchen,' Mrs Templeton announced. 'Coffee, Storm?'

'Yes, please. I'll give you a hand with the trolley.'

'You won't escape that way, my girl,' warned her father. 'We'll thrash this out later. Think a little, love. The man's got a job to do, don't go out of your way to make it any harder for him. He's going to need all the help he can get.'

'Not according to what one reads in the papers,' Storm

retorted. 'To read them you'd think he was a one-man miracle worker!'

Over her downbent head her parents exchanged exasperatedly affectionate looks.

'There's a documentary on television I wouldn't mind seeing tonight,' Mr Templeton announced, changing the subject.

Storm followed her mother out into the kitchen.

'Your father's right, you know, dear,' Mrs Templeton said gently as they washed up. 'You mustn't let loyalty to David blind you to his faults.' She gave a faint sigh. 'I know it's none of my business, Storm, but somehow I can't see David as the right man for you . . .'

'Because he's gentle and kind and doesn't have sex on the brain?' Storm retorted fiercely, causing her mother to frown anxiously.

'I know you think you love him, Storm,' she said quietly, 'but if you did I should expect you to want him to have "sex on the brain", as you put it. Things were different in my day, I know, and sex wasn't discussed as openly as it is now, but there was never a single doubt in my mind that I wanted your father as my lover, very, very much indeed. I don't think you can say the same about David.'

This unexpected frankness brought a touch of colour to Storm's face.

'Too much importance is placed on sex,' she announced defensively. 'It's only one part of a relationship.'

'The mere fact that you can tell me that, Storm,' her mother replied softly, 'just confirms what I've been saying. You can't possibly love David as a woman should love a man.'

Her mother was hopelessly romantic, Storm thought as she finished her chores, but even so her words lingered, making it impossible for Storm to concentrate on the documentary. When it had finished Mrs Templeton announced suddenly,

'I forget to tell you—the house down the road has been sold.'

'Good lord!' Mr Templeton exclaimed. 'I never thought it would go so quickly. How much were they asking for it? Well over a hundred thousand, wasn't it?'

The house in question was their nearest neighbour, the last word in modern design and yet built in such a fashion that it blended perfectly into its rural surroundings. Much use had been made of huge expanses of tinted glass and natural wood. The house had extensive grounds and overlooked the wooded copse that lay between Storm's parents' house and it, and Mrs Templeton, who had been inside it, said that it was as beautiful inside as it was out.

'Going out with David tonight?' Mrs Templeton asked Storm a little later.

'No. He's got some work to do, and so have I.'

'Making sure the new boss doesn't catch you off guard?' grinned her father.

Storm elected to take refuge from his teasing in a disdainful demeanour.

'Certainly not. I couldn't care less what Jago Marsh thinks of me!'

But she could not get away from the fact that hateful though he might be, Jago Marsh was going to be in a position of authority over her, and worse still, capable of taking from her a job which she thoroughly enjoyed and had worked hard for.

It was an unpalatable thought to take to bed, and she was unusually quiet when she said her goodnights. Upstairs in her room she dawdled over her preparations for bed, stopping to lean her elbows on her casement window and stare out at the night sky.

Why of all people had David had to confide in Jago Marsh? her rebellious heart demanded, her inner eye seeing him as he had appeared to her during his lecture.

He had been wearing a tailored suit, his dark hair neatly brushed, outwardly a conformist adhering to the rules of society, but his face had been that of a man who admits to no rules, except his own; a man who would either lead the pack or turn his back on it; a man who in her heart of hearts she acknowledged was dangerous.

She vowed there and then that when the confrontation came, he would not find her unprepared.

CHAPTER TWO

IT was to come far sooner than she had expected.

The day had not got off to an auspicious start. Far from it, Storm thought as she tussled with a recalcitrant zip. She had overslept, and the fact that she had an important appointment with the managing director of a Gloucester-based employment agency whom she had hoped to persuade to make use of the station's advertising facilities made her all fingers and thumbs as she pulled on a pale grey skirt and a toning lavender blouse.

The blouse was startlingly effective against her hair, reflecting the colour of her eyes as she blended subtly shaded mauve eyeshadow over her eyelids, adding the merest touch of mascara and kohl pencil, before snatching up her fox jacket—a combined twenty-first birthday present from her parents and brothers. At least the fur gave her a touch of elegance, she thought ruefully as she applied damson lip gloss—something she considered herself badly in need of. She studied herself in the mirror, frowning a little. Thank goodness for high heels! Five foot two did not make for the soignée model girl elegance she envied so much. Her lack of inches was a constant source of irritation to her. 'Titch' and 'Pint Size' were only two of the derogatory names used by her brothers during their adolescence, and to add insult to injury they took after their father, easily topping six foot!

Conditioned to her spectacular colouring, Storm was oblivious to the vivid effect of her russet curls against the creamy warmth of her skin, or the generously full curve of her mouth beneath its covering of lip gloss. Wrinkling her nose, she picked up her bag and fled. She was late enough already without wasting more time staring at her own reflection.

Breakfast was a hurried affair, with her mother scolding her affectionately as she swallowed her coffee and refused anything more substantial. Mrs Templeton was lending Storm her Mini and, as always when time was short, this temperamental dowager refused to start first time.

'She *won't* start if you speak to her like that,' Mrs Templeton warned Storm who was muttering curses over the Mini's obstinacy. 'She's an old lady and it's a cold morning.'

Storm grinned. Her mother's habit of treating her elderly car as an eccentric member of the family was a standing joke.

'Don't worry,' she promised, 'I'll pay due consideration to her advancing years and uncertain health!'

Very little traffic used the winding road to Gloucester. The early morning mist had dispersed, leaving only the odd patch here and there in low-lying hollows. The glinting autumn sun sparkled on frost-rimed hedges, and Storm hummed happily as she drove along.

Later she admitted to herself that she had been guilty of letting her mind wander, and perhaps even taking up more than her allotted half share of the road, but that was later. Her first instinctive reaction when she saw the powerful green car leaping towards her devouring the slender distance that separated them was one of furious resentment that its driver should behave with such a lack of regard for any other road users.

With almost unbelievable speed the other car swerved away, narrowly missing her, and as Storm glared revengefully at its occupants, she realised that the man seated in the passenger seat was Neil Philips, the local estate agent. Which meant that in all probability the driver was none other than their new neighbour. Scarcely a good omen for their future relationship Storm admitted as she gave the Mini's steering wheel a reassuring pat. Really, she was getting quite as bad as her mother! A car was a car was a car! Unless, of course, it happened to be an expensive luxury toy designed for men rich and vain enough to own such objects, she reflected, remembering the sleek lines of the green monster. She tossed her head. Arrogant brute, to sound his horn like that! He had been as much in the wrong as she was!

But she had not been giving her driving the concentration she ought to have done, she admitted. Her mind had been on Jago Marsh and the difference his coming was bound to make to her life. David had not said when they might expect him, but surely it would take some time for him to tie up his business affairs in London; that should give them a little breathing space.

Gloucester was busy. It took her ten minutes to find a parking space and another five to check her hair and make-up before sliding out of the car and hurrying towards the Top Girl agency. That was one thing, she thought, chuckling to herself, at least being small meant that one could get out of a Mini without tying oneself in knots.

She made an attractive picture, her skirt toning perfectly with the fox jacket, her hair a banner of rich colour against the pale subtlety of the fur, her eyes shining with anticipation. Several passers-by stopped to give her a second look, but Storm barely noticed.

The clock was just striking ten when she pushed open the plate-glass door of the modern office block which housed the agency's offices. Disappointment awaited her. The man she had come to see had been called to an urgent meeting in Banbury, and had had to cancel their appointment.

His secretary was sympathetic, offering Storm a cup of coffee as she explained that she had tried to reach her at Radio Wyechester without success.

Storm fought to quell her disappointment. She had worked hard to secure this appointment and had come prepared with various suggestions for alternative jingles and themes that could be used to promote the agency. She suspected that the head of the agency had only agreed to their appointment because she had pressed him, and had in fact been relieved to find an excuse to cancel. However, she had learned that in advertising confidence was everything, so she composed her features into a relaxed smile, and got out her diary to make a fresh appointment.

A whole morning wasted, she thought miserably an hour later as she parked her car in the supermarket car-park beneath their offices. As usual it was crowded, and because Sam Townley refused to give them permanent car-parking spaces she had to circle it a couple of times before she could find a gap. Feeling unusually hot and bothered, she headed for the studio.

Sue stopped her in the outer office.

'Message for you.' She pulled a face. 'Your friend Mr Beton's been on. He says his ad was cut short again last night, and that it was indistinct. He wants to know if you're going to cut his bill to match.'

'Damn!' Storm swore feelingly. 'I'll give him a ring later on. Anything else?'

Sue shook her head. 'No other messages, but David wants to see you. He said to go to his office the moment you arrived. Pete and the others are already there.'

'Okay. I'll be right there,' Storm told her. David must have decided to hold a meeting following on from his visit to London. Perhaps he wanted to plan a campaign to show Jago Marsh that they weren't a total write-off. She certainly hoped so.

When she slipped into David's office five minutes later, there was an atmosphere of tense expectancy in the air. Pete, who was standing nearest to the door, draped an arm across her shoulder, pulling her against him.

David's small office was cramped at the best of times, but with three of their four technicians, Pete, David himself and Storm in it, there was barely room to move without breathing in, and in vain Storm craned her neck to see over the taller male heads.

'What's up? Frightened you'll miss something, my lovely?' Pete teased, mocking her lack of inches.

It wasn't often that Storm lost her cool with her colleagues, but the irritations of the morning had mounted up and her temper was at boiling point. Now it spilled over, making her snap back angrily,

'What's to miss, for heaven's sake? I could do without another eulogy on the marvels performed by Mr Magnificent Marsh. I know David's desperately trying to sweeten the pill and all credit to him, but as far as I'm concerned Jago Marsh is still poison!'

There was an uncomfortable silence and Storm realised that her voice had carried farther than she had intended. She was just about to mumble an apology for interrupting the meeting when a voice far cooler and crisper than David's mild tones drawled sapiently from the other side of the room,

'Ah, I see our missing Advertising Controller has condescended to join us. Perhaps if you took the trouble to listen occasionally, Miss Templeton, instead of commandeering the conversation you might learn something. Marvels, as you call them, aren't achieved simply by waving a magic wand. They take time and hard work— something that appears to be conspicuously lacking in this set-up.'

Her cheeks burned.

'Naughty, naughty!' Pete whispered in her ear. 'You've pulled the tiger's tail with a vengeance, my lovely. I do believe he's about to make an example of you!'

As though by magic a path had cleared to David's desk,

and for the first time Storm had an uninterrupted view of the man lounging there.

She recognised him immediately. There was no-mistaking that tall well-muscled body encased in an immaculate charcoal-grey suit, nor the hard-boned masculine profile, icy-grey eyes sweeping her from head to foot.

Jago Marsh! Here already! She could hardly believe it.

He flicked back a crisp white shirt cuff to glance meaningfully at the gold Rollex watch strapped to his wrist, and Storm stifled her resentment. If he was trying to imply that she was late for work, he would soon learn different. He came out from behind his desk, the suggestion of restrained power very evident in his lithe movements, his black hair slightly longer than she had remembered, brushing the collar of his jacket. He gestured to the chair in front of David's desk and said in a deceptively calm voice:

'Sit down, Storm.'

Every instinct warned her that here was a man who was dangerous. She tried to keep calm, forcing herself to meet his eyes. They were dark grey and right at this moment looked uncommonly like the North Sea when an east wind was blowing over it. She was half way towards the chair before she realised what she was doing, and straightened abruptly. 'I'll stand, thank you,' she said clearly. 'I'm no different from the other members of this team. Just because I'm female I don't expect to be treated any differently.'

And he could take that whichever way he chose, she decided triumphantly.

For several unnerving seconds she was forced to endure the diamond brilliance of ice-cold scrutiny and then he was smiling derisively.

'Well, you're right about one thing,' he drawled coolly. 'You're feminine all right.'

To her chagrin the others, including David, laughed.

Her whole body was quivering with indignation, but even so she was completely unprepared for the hard hands descending on her shoulders as she was propelled backwards and forced gently into the chair.

'There,' Jago said gently. 'Now you can both see and hear what's going on and everyone else can see over you.'

Storm's cheeks burned anew. He made her sound like a spoiled, fractious child! Beneath her blouse her skin felt as though it were on fire where he had touched her, her emotions in chaos.

'Now,' he drawled, 'I'll continue, and if it makes it any easier for you, I promise you I'm not here to dwell on past glories—mine or anyone else's.' His eyes swept the room. 'There's one thing for sure, if we were relying on relating the successes of your venture we'd have precious little to talk about.'

Here it came, Storm thought numbly. How he must be gloating! Barging in among them, wearing clothes more suitable to a boardroom than David's shabby office. All that she was feeling showed in her eyes, as she lifted them to his unreadable face. He returned the look, his eyes dropping to the soft curves so lightly masked by the lavender silk blouse. Without a trace of embarrassment they lingered for a while before making a full and appreciative study of the rest of her body, and when his eyes eventually returned to her face, they were no longer cold but warmly sensual with a meaning that was distinctly plain.

Storm went hot and then cold, trying to appear unaffected by the blatantly sensual inspection. No one had ever looked at her like that before, and she shivered a little without knowing why.

'Well, Storm?' he queried in the silence which followed. 'You seemed to have plenty to say for yourself earlier on, suppose you tell me why after nearly twelve months' operation you're still floundering about like a bunch of amateurs, playing at operating a radio station.'

That disturbing sexually aware look might never have been, his voice and eyes probed mercilessly, driving her to murmur defiantly under her breath,

'Perhaps it's because we can't all aspire to the dizzy heights surmounted by the Jago Marshes of this world.'

She hadn't intended him to hear, but when his mouth tightened comprehendingly she knew that he had.

She quaked inwardly as he advanced on her with a lithe cat-like tread, but she had come too far to back down now. She was not susceptible enough to be reduced to jelly by a mere look, she reminded herself, her chin lifting proudly as she waited for his acid denunciation.

However, it seemed he had more control of his temper than she had of hers, for he merely looked at her rather thoughtfully before commenting softly,

'Since you appear so keen on airing you views, Storm, perhaps you'd care to favour us with an explanation of these advertising figures.'

She'd been wrong about his temper, Storm thought, as he thrust a file under her nose. It was there all right; smouldering in the look he gave her, reminding her of what he thought of women in the media. An unpleasant thought struck her. Perhaps he was deliberately trying to goad her into handing in her notice. Well, she wouldn't fall for that one, she decided grimly as he dropped the file on David's desk, his eyes never leaving her face.

'Barely a thousand pounds a week in revenues. In London we turn over fifty thousand in exactly the same time span, and that's allowing only six minutes of commercials to the hour. It turns the listeners off if they're swamped by commercial breaks. Those aren't what they tune in for, but I'm sure all this is merely coals to New-castle as far as you're concerned, Storm. What,' his eyebrows arched in unconcealed contempt, 'nothing to say for yourself?'

As she fought for self-control she heard David interrupt placatingly, 'Storm is highly qualified and very experienced, Jago. She was with an excellent advertising agency in Oxford before she joined us . . .'

'Really?' The cool reply came dubiously, the hard eyes probing. 'She looks very young to be . . . experienced.'

Damn the man! Storm thought savagely, reacting instinctively to the deliberate taunt.

'I know you don't approve of women in the media, Mr Marsh,' she said as calmly as she could. 'And please don't bother to deny it, I've heard you lecture on the subject. But there's such a thing as equal opportunities these days, and I intend to prove that I can do this job as well as any man. Now, about these figures.' Not daring to look at him or to allow herself to dwell on the silence which had fallen on the room, she picked up the advertising file, shuffling the papers to conceal how nervous she felt. Reaction was beginning to set in, but she could not back down now. She had taken her stand and must prove to Jago Marsh once and for all that while she might be a woman as far as her work went she expected to be treated in the same manner as he would treat a male colleague, and not be subjected to the covert sexual warfare he had been indulging in before.

'Firstly,' she told him, striving to keep her voice even and calm, 'Wyechester isn't London and people—life moves at a much slower pace. It takes time to convince local businessmen to make use of our services and . . .'

'I'll say it does!' Jago cut in contemptuously, without letting her finish. 'But how much time do you need? Time is something you're running out of here,' he reminded them curtly. 'That's why I'm here, to try and put things right before the I.B.A. are left with no option but to blow the whistle on the entire venture.'

'How very generous of you!' Storm interrupted sarcastically, before she could stop herself.

Jago inclined his head, and the look he gave her held an implicit promise of retribution to come. Storm couldn't help herself, her eyes dropped, her cheeks flushing with mortification. In the silence that followed it would have been possible to hear the proverbial pin drop.

'I was warned that you were something of a firebrand, Storm,' Jago said smoothly. 'Well, let me tell you here and now if there are going to be any fireworks in this outfit, they're going to originate from me, and they're more likely to take the form of a rocket under your backside unless I see a drastic improvement.'

'Doesn't mince matters, does he?' Pete murmured with an appreciative chuckle, but Storm did not bother to reply. All her attention was focused on the man facing her across David's desk.

'Is that understood?' Jago asked. 'Good.' The cool grey eyes summed up their reaction, resting momentarily on Storm's openly rebellious face. 'A word of warning, Storm, before you get any idiotic ideas into your head—I have ways of turning firecrackers into damp squibs.'

'I'll just bet you have!' Pete grinned appreciatively, while to Storm's fury all the men with the exception of David laughed out loud. Closing ranks against the female in their midst, she thought resentfully, only her clenched hands betraying her feelings as she tried to appear both cool and unmoved.

'I thought you'd come here to show us how to run the station at a profit, not reform my character,' she riposted lightly, when the laughter had died down. Let *him* see how it felt to be the object of everyone's amusement!

He was watching her with a thoughtful narrowed gaze that made her heart thump uncomfortably and warned her that she had gone too far, then his expression lightened, amusement glinting in his eyes.

'I'm perfectly capable of doing both,' he assured her smoothly, an inflection in the words that sent a frisson of awareness shivering over her skin.

The others laughed again, but in Storm's mind there was no doubt that the glove had been most definitely thrown down. But did she dare to pick it up? Some instinct more deep-rooted than any ordinary emotion warned her that to do so would be dangerous. And yet what had she to lose? Her job and her pride were surely more important to her than that.

'In fact,' Jago mused, his eyes on her slender curves, 'I'm not sure if I won't anyway. Taming shrews can sometimes have the most unexpected fringe benefits.'

This time there was no laughter. She caught David's eye in a mute plea for help, willing him to tell Jago Marsh that if there was any taming to be done *he* was the one who would be doing it. But of course David would do no such thing, she acknowledged, and wasn't it precisely because he would not that she loved him?

'Perhaps if you could tear yourself away from your daydream, Storm?'

Engrossed in her thoughts, she had missed part of the conversation. The others were all looking expectantly at her, and she ran her tongue nervously round her dry lips.

'Well?' Jago prompted softly. 'We're all waiting. Perhaps you could enlighten us as to exactly why Radio Wyechester is such a resounding failure?'

How could David endure to stand there and listen to him? Storm wondered resentfully.

'I agree that we have a long way to go,' she began, intending to mention the decrepit state of some of their equipment, but Jago stopped her, saying dryly.

'I'm glad we agree on something, but you certainly believe in the understatement, don't you? For "a long way", I would substitute "all the way". You haven't even taken the first step in the right direction.'

'But no doubt we will, under your capable tutelage!' Storm shot back resentfully.

Jago inclined his head briefly as though in assent. His eyes bored into her.

'It's to be hoped so,' he agreed. 'Now, if I can have your attention for a moment, all of you. The first thing we need to know before you can become a success is why you're at present a failure.' He looked round the room, ignoring Storm's rebellious disdain.

He certainly had a way of delivering a snub that was all his own, she had to acknowledge seconds later when his eyes returned to her flushed face, and lingered, looking straight through her, while the others shuffled uncomfortably and looked at one another for support. Why didn't David say something? Storm wondered helplessly. Surely he had formulated some defence for the attack which he must have known would be coming? Surely he wasn't going to let Jago Marsh sweep in here and simply take over? But it certainly looked that way.

'I'm going to take five days to look round and see what's to be done and then I shall hold a round-the-table meeting to get your views,' Jago told them crisply when no one spoke.

'Five days—is that all?' Storm muttered under her breath, willing David to defend their venture and himself. 'Even God took six!'

'You can go now,' Jago told them coolly, gathering up his papers. 'All except you, Storm. I have something to say to you—in private,' he added, as David showed signs of lingering.

Storm held her breath waiting for David to tell Jago that anything he had to say to her in private could be said to him, but to her dismay he merely gave her a sympathetic smile before following the others out of the office.

'Well now,' said Jago when they were alone, 'that's quite an act you've got together there. Want to tell me why?'

'What did you expect?' Storm asked dangerously. 'I

know your views on women in the media, and I hate the way you're pushing David about. Well, as far as I'm concerned, he's still Controller here and I take my orders from him.'

'I'll bet,' Jago drawled cynically. 'The day David Winters can bring himself to give an order—that I've got to see!'

'Don't you criticise David! He's worth ten of you.'

'Not so far as the I.B.A. are concerned.'

Impossible to deny the truth of that statement, much as she would have wanted to. Angry tears weren't far away, and Storm blinked them back.

'All this concern, and for old David! I'm impressed.' The derogatory tones could not be ignored, and drawing herself up to her full height, Storm choked back:

'Why shouldn't I be concerned for him? I happen to be in love with him!'

She must surely have imagined the incredulity in those narrowed grey eyes, she told herself seconds later, when it had been banished to be replaced with a satirical smile. 'Are you indeed? You do surprise me.'

His tone caught her off guard, making her say defensively, 'You find it hard to believe that David could love me?'

'Not particularly that he could,' came the ambiguous response, 'but that he has. He certainly hasn't taught you to purr instead of scratch,' he added contemplatively, his eyes assessing her stiffening body.

'So you're in love with David. Do you sleep together?'

The question threw her, making her colour vividly. 'What does it matter if we do?' she asked breathlessly. 'Our relationship doesn't affect our work, if that's what you're implying.'

'I can see that. He'd have let me tear you to pieces back there, wouldn't he? He's not the man for you, Storm,' Jago said softly. 'He'll never tame you . . .'

'I don't want to be tamed!' Storm told him defiantly, her eyes widening as she realised what she had betrayed.

Jago watched her. 'So that's it. You don't love David,' he told her positively, 'you're using him as a means of keeping your feelings in cold storage. Well, you can't do that for ever.'

'Who's going to stop me?' Storm responded angrily, wondering how she had allowed herself to be manoeuvred on to this dangerous subject. 'You?'

There was a tiny pause when she wished as she had never wished for anything in her life before that she had not added that foolish, challenging word, and then, observing the satisfaction gleaming in the grey eyes watching her, knew that she had been deliberately goaded into it.

'Why not?' Jago drawled smoothly, his fingers reaching out to brush the curls back from her cheek. Even that light touch was enough to make Storm back nervously away from him, her defences alerted to the danger he represented.

'Don't touch me!' she choked fiercely, but he merely laughed, and moved towards her, his eyes lingering on the rapid rise and fall of her breasts beneath their thin covering of silk.

'If you really are in love with David, my touch won't have any power to affect you, will it?' he murmured logically, his eyes almost mesmerising her. 'But you don't love him, do you, Storm?'

'Of course I do!' she protested. 'Why are you doing this to me? Why can't you leave me alone?'

'Why? Because you're an extremely desirable young woman, with a body that excites me. I want you, Storm,' he told her suddenly, shocking her with the baldness of his statement. 'And what I want, I get.'

'Well, I don't want you!' Storm protested vehemently,

emotion darkening her eyes to the colour of pansies. 'I love David.'

Jago looked at her for a moment and in his eyes she saw the determination of a man used to getting his own way. It took all the self control she had at her command to hold that gaze.

'You're a liar,' he told her, 'on both counts, and before too long I'll prove it to you.'

'I'm going straight to David to tell him what you've just said!' Storm told him furiously, but the steely grip of his fingers on her arms sliced off her protests, his eyes dark as they bored into hers.

'You do just that,' he told her softly, 'and you'll find out exactly how little your precious David cares about you. Once he knows I want you he'll drop you like a hot potato. All David Winters wants from life is peace and quiet, and if he thinks letting me have you will get it for him, he'd wrap you up himself in pretty paper and hand hand you over tied up in pink ribbons.'

'I hate you!' Storm breathed, trembling with indignation. 'David would never . . .'

Her protest was silenced as hard male lips claimed her mouth, her body drawn against masculine contours and she was forced to endure an intimacy of touch she had always previously avoided. She stiffened within the embrace, her mouth closing stubbornly as she refused to respond.

Jago laughed softly.

'You've got a lot to learn, Storm Templeton,' he told her mockingly, 'but I shall enjoy teaching you.'

'I loathe you!' Storm spat at him, pulling herself out of his arms.

He made no attempt to follow her, his expression thoughtfully assessing as it lingered on her dilated eyes.

'You fear me,' he corrected, startling her with his insight. 'And you fear the emotions I might arouse, isn't that more to the point? Is that why you chose David? Because he was nice and safe?'

'You've no right to question me about my private life,' Storm protested, fumbling with the door. 'And whatever you may choose to think of your prowess, you do nothing for me.'

'But I shall.' Jago promised softly as she fled. 'Believe me, Storm, I shall.'

Her first instinct was to go straight to David and tell him what had happened, but the tiny kernel of truth in Jago's statement would not be denied. David hated trouble of any kind, and while she did not believe for one moment that he would 'hand her over' as Jago had suggested—she was not David's possession, after all—she knew that he would probably try and reason her out of her present frame of mind, explaining away Jago's comments as a form of teasing, or worse still a product of her imagination. She had always approved of his lack of jealousy, she reminded herself, so it was hardly fair now to wish that he might tell Jago in no uncertain terms that she belonged to him. Anyway, she had no need of David to defend her. Surely she was perfectly capable of telling Jago herself that he did not interest her? But somehow she had an idea that he wouldn't take 'no' for an answer.

She could still not quite believe that it had all happened. One moment they had been discussing work and the next ... But no, that was not true, she acknowledged. From the moment he had looked at her in that disturbingly sensual manner she had known that he desired her. It had happened before and she had not felt the tremulous fear she felt now. But Jago Marsh was like no man she had ever known before, she acknowledged, and something deep inside her reacted to him whether she liked it or not. He aroused in her a primitive fear she had never known before, panicking her into all manner of foolish reactions. She would just have to strive to appear cool and in control of the situation, she told herself. Men like Jago Marsh did not normally have to work very hard to secure their sexual pleasures and doubtless once he realised that she did not intend to play ball, he would drop her and pursue someone else.

The shock of seeing him there in David's office this morning had made her more vulnerable than she would normally be, but from now on she would be on her guard. He might desire her, but so what? an inner voice asked sardonically. She herself had said that he changed his girl-friends as frequently as he changed his shirts, and no doubt the sophisticated crowd he moved in thought no more of going to bed with someone than they did of shaking hands—possibly even less.

He was still on her mind later in the day when she left the studio, and she grimaced a little at her own stupidity in allowing him to monopolise so much of her attention as she unlocked the Mini. If Jago Marsh thought she was going to be another easy conquest, he had better think again. She loved David and would continue to do so. But did David love her? There had never been any mention of an engagement or marriage. David had never even held her in the way that Jago had this morning, making her intensely aware of the fact that he was entirely male and doing it quite deliberately. She had never felt the faintest sexual stirring in his arms, but then wasn't that what she had wanted? So why did she suddenly long for David to sweep her off her feet and make love to her until she was irrevocably committed, and safely beyond the reach of Jago Marsh?

CHAPTER THREE

FIVE days Jago had given them, and no five days had ever passed so swiftly. In fact they were so hectic that Storm barely saw David, except to exchange a few brief words of conversation in passing. She had noticed, though, that he seemed very subdued and she was glad she had not burdened him with her own problems. His stoop seemed to have become even more pronounced, but instead of filling her with compassion, his defeatist attitude made her long to tell him to fight back, to show Jago that he was equally capable of running the station.

As far as the others were concerned David might as well have ceased to exist as Controller. Jago had been accepted with a wholehearted approval that grated on Storm's raw nerves. She was beginning to feel like the last surviving victim of a cataclysm. Everyone apart from herself seemed to have succumbed to Jago's cool charm, and even David deferred to him quite willingly. Sue and Janet, the two office girls, were already mooning over their new boss's good looks; Pete mentioned his name with every other breath, and talked unceasingly of his hopes that their connections with Jago might lead to a D.J. spot for him in London, and even the technicians were full of praise for the man whom Storm still thought of as an intruder.

Never had she been so thankful to see a Friday. Halfway through the morning the Beton tape had jammed, and the result was that Storm was trying to placate a furious Mr Beton with the promise that his ad would get double time in the afternoon.

She was with the technicians waiting for their verdict

on how long it would be before the tape could be run when Ken, the younger of the two, piped up admiringly:

'You should have seen Jago this morning, Storm. We were having problems with the stereo output, and he located the fault in about ten seconds flat. Said it was easy after nearly fifteen years in the business. You'd never get David doing anything like that.'

Stung into David's defence, Storm said sarcastically: 'Perhaps I ought to take this tape to him, then. Did no one ever warn you about worshipping graven images, young Ken?'

'And did no one ever warn you about making snide remarks where they could be overheard?' Jago drawled from her shoulder.

He had come in so quietly that Storm had not heard him. She spun round, her body reacting instantly to his presence, alarm feathering along her nerves. She had been working too hard, she told herself as she felt an inner tremor; that was all. Her nerves were on edge from the strain she had been under.

Jago ignored her, crouching down beside Ken, murmuring a few words of advice while Storm waited for her tape.

'What's the matter?' Jago drawled, when Ken handed it to her. 'Spoiled the nice picture you had built up of me, have I? What did you think I was? I was mending tapes like these when you were still in your pram. You complain about the equipment you have here. You should have seen the stuff we had on board the old *Cynthia*. And by the way,' he added, his eyes merciless as they scrutinised her pale face, 'the next time you feel like criticising me, have the guts to do it to my face.'

He was gone before she could retort, leaving her trembling with nervous reaction and other emotions she found it impossible to name.

She mustn't let him get to her like this, she told herself as she took the tape back to the studio. She must never forget that they were engaged upon a war and the moment she let him overpower her she would have lost it.

She was just about to telephone Mr Beton when Sue came in.

'Jago wants to see you,' she said breathlessly, her expression envious.

He had taken over David's office—just as he had taken over David's job, Storm thought rebelliously as she knocked on the door and walked in.

Jago was studying some papers, which he dropped on to the desk, reminding her that he wanted to see her to go over the advertising figures first thing on Tuesday morning. Was he actually giving her time to prepare her case? she asked herself acidly. Munificence indeed!

'Something wrong?' he asked coolly, leaning back in his chair—David's chair really, Storm thought angrily. When she didn't answer an understanding smile quivered across his mouth.

'Ah yes, I see what it is,' he drawled. 'Poor Storm, what did you expect? A torrid love scene in the office? Been nerving yourself to fight me off, have you?'

He was on his feet, standing behind her, so close that Storm could feel his warm breath stirring her hair. Just being in the same room with him seemed to drain her energy and yet fill her with a claustrophobic fear at the same time. He hadn't made the slightest move to touch her in any way, but she was more intensely aware of his maleness than she would have been had she felt his hard body pressed against her own.

'I never mix business with pleasure,' Storm heard him say. 'Don't worry, though. When I'm ready to make love to you, you'll know all about it. Have dinner with me tonight?' he asked unexpectedly. He saw the warning flash in her eyes and laughed. 'David is going to Oxford—on business,' he told her softly, 'so don't go running to him for help.'

'I wouldn't have dinner with you if . . . if I were starving!' she managed disdainfully as she thrust open the door. Surely he must know how much she disliked him? But then of course feeling would never matter to Jago Marsh. She was simply an appetite he wanted to appease, and once he had done so, she would be tossed on one side—discarded. But she would make sure that would never happen!

Back in her own cubbyhole of an office she buzzed through to Sue and asked if she knew where David was.

'Gone out,' came the other girl's cheerful response. 'Didn't he tell you?'

There hadn't been time to tell one another very much lately, Storm thought uneasily. She and David normally went out together on Friday evenings and he had said nothing to her about visiting Oxford, although she knew he had friends living there from his university days.

'Doing anything tonight?'

She hadn't heard Pete come in, and he perched on the edge of her desk grinning down at her.

'And don't tell me you're going out with old David, because I know you're not. Told me himself that he was going away for the weekend.'

It seemed that David had told everyone but her, Storm thought a little resentfully. Her phone rang and she moved to pick it up, covering the receiver as Pete coaxed, 'Come on, we'll go and have a drink with the crowd. Strictly platonic, I promise.'

She didn't feel much like an evening at home, she admitted, acknowledging the growing restlessness she had experienced over the last few days. An evening out would do her good.

'Pick me up at nine,' she mouthed to Pete, who nodded and gave her a mock salute as he left.

Later in the afternoon she felt so tired that she half

regretted her decision to go out, but it was too late to change her mind. Her father had offered to collect her from work, and he was waiting in the car-park when Storm got outside.

The fields were a patchwork of varying greens and golds, broken by the odd spot of dark brown where the earth had been turned for a winter crop, cobbled together with the neat grey lines of the dry-stone walls. Storm lay back in her seat and closed her eyes.

'You're quiet.' Mr Templeton shot her an amused look. 'Finding this new boss harder to handle than old David?'

'David isn't old!' Storm expostulated, but Mr Templeton just grinned.

'Some people are born old, my girl, and some are always young. Your David is one of the former, and you, my love, are most definitely one of the latter.'

Irreverently Storm wondered into which category Jago Marsh fell, squashing the admission that he was a man it would be virtually impossible to define or put into a pre-cast mould, and then dismissed him firmly from her mind and gave her attention exclusively to her father.

'Going out with David tonight?' he asked quizzically.

Storm shook her head. 'He's in Oxford.' No need to tell her father that David had neglected to inform her of his intentions. 'I'm going out with Pete and the usual crowd, just for a drink.'

'Do you good,' Mr Templeton approved. 'You've been rather preoccupied lately. Care to talk about it?'

'There's nothing to talk about,' Storm replied rather huskily. That was the beauty of her parents, although they never interfered they were always ready and willing to listen to her problems and suggest a solution.

She smiled a little wryly at the thought of her father's reaction to the information that Jago Marsh wanted to make her his mistress. If one could apply such an outdated word to the undoubtedly ephemeral relationship he had in mind. Knowing her father's love of logic he would probably have some perfectly rational explanation for the other man's behaviour, Storm reflected with a sigh. This was one problem she could not share with her parents, although she admitted that perhaps some self-analysis was called for.

Her mind shied away from the admission. Just because Jago Marsh made her feel nervous . . . threatened. It was a perfectly natural reaction and one that any girl would have felt faced with his coolly stated intentions. She had no desire to become involved in any purely sexual relationship. Mutual respect; shared interests—these were the things on which durable relationships were formed.

She heard the familiar toot of Pete's car horn while she was putting on her make-up. The crowd Pete mixed with were essentially a casual lot; so Storm had donned tight-fitting black cord jeans, topped with a silky white blouse with a yoke that emphasised the fullness of her breasts and full sleeves gathered into a tight cuff. A brief matching cord waistcoat drew attention to her slim waist, giving her an almost mediaeval air, and as she applied her eyeshadow with a practised hand she heard Pete cheerfully returning her mother's greeting.

Peach blusher highlighted her cheekbones, and a shiny lip gloss emphasised the sensuous curve of her mouth. She brushed her hair quickly, then slipped on her knee-length suede boots, zipping them closed.

'Fancy dress, is it?' her father asked teasingly when she opened the door, while Mrs Templeton enquired plaintively, 'Oh, Storm, why don't you wear one of your pretty dresses? You look like a boy!'

'Not from where I'm standing she doesn't,' Pete announced with so much relish that Storm's parents laughed. 'Ready?'

Storm nodded.

'Something sure smells nice,' Pete commented as he opened the passenger door of his small sports car for her.

'Last birthday's Chanel Number Five. A present from John,' Storm told him. 'Thank heavens for big brothers!'

'As long as they don't loom too protectively,' Pete grinned as he slid behind the steering wheel.

It wasn't very far to the pub favoured by Pete's cronies, and although he drove his small car at a speed that some might have thought a little excessive, Storm knew that he was a reliable driver.

The car-park was full, and Pete let her out by the pub door while he found somewhere to leave the car. when he joined her and ushered her inside they were greeted with cheers and cries of delight by their friends.

'Long time no see,' one of the girls commented to Storm. 'Is it all over with you and David?'

Storm didn't have time to reply. Pete was asking what she wanted to drink and she asked for a dry Martini. She wasn't particularly fond of strong alcohol, and usually found one drink lasted her all evening.

'What's up, Storm?' one of the others asked when they had all got their drinks and were seated round one of the tables. 'You're unusually quiet.'

'It's a case of an immovable object meeting an irresistible force,' Pete joked.

Everyone laughed, and one of the boys said admiringly:

'I'd like to meet the immovable object, then!'

Storm ignored their banter.

The pub originated from Tudor times and had recently been tastefully modernised by the brewery. During the renovations the builders had uncovered some of the original oak beams and a huge stone fireplace, which had now been incorporated into the decor. The result was extremely effective. Horse brasses glinted in the crackling flames from the fire, giving the room an air of cosy intimacy, and Storm stretched out her hands, revelling in its warmth. A movement by the door caught her eye and she heard Pete murmur softly;

'I think your wish is about to be granted, Rick. Unless I'm mistaken here's our immovable object.' He rose, thrusting his glass into Storm's hand. 'Hang on to this, lovely. Our august boss has just walked in. I'll go over and ask him to join us. Give the girls a thrill anyway.'

He winked and was gone before Storm had the chance to protest. The bar was filling up quickly and when Pete returned with Jago Marsh at his side, the only spare seat was a tapestry-covered stool at Storm's side.

She acknowledged Jago's general greeting with a tight smile. If she'd known there was the slightest chance that he might appear she would never have come. He was wearing close-fitting dark trousers and an open-necked shirt. His pants moulded the narrow outline of his hips, emphasising the muscled tautness of his thighs. Storm looked away, more shaken by his presence than she wanted to admit. He sat down next to her and she ignored him, engaging the girl on her right in conversation. When Pete called her name she looked up, thinking he was going to ask her if she wanted another drink.

'Bob and Sheila have just come in,' he said instead. 'How about perching on my knee so that they'll have somewhere to sit?'

Some of the girls were already sitting with their boyfriends and, not wanting to be thought awkward, Storm got up. Pete was sitting on the opposite side of the glass-cluttered table and as she started to edge gingerly past the empty glasses, Jago's fingers clamped determinedly round her wrist.

'Use my knee, Storm,' he said in a deceptively mild voice. 'I'd hate you to have to pay for all those glasses.'

The others laughed. Storm looked at Pete, willing him to come to her rescue, but all his attention was on a particularly attractive blonde standing by the bar.

'Give in gracefully,' Jago murmured against Storm's ear. 'Pete isn't going to help.'

'Why did you have to come here?' she began angrily, silenced by the sudden glint in Jago's eyes, as his grip tightened and he pulled her against him, forcing her to accede to his wishes and perch herself, rather gingerly, on his lap.

She could feel the hard muscles of his thighs even through her own jeans and edged furtively away, alarm licking through her veins. There had been dozens of occasions when she had sat like this with a boy, but never, ever had she felt as vulnerable as she did right now.

'If the mountain won't come to Mahomet,' Jago murmured, responding to her earlier question, laughing a little as her eyes widened in comprehension.

'You mean you deliberately came here?' she breathed, trying to catch Pete's eye. Had he known all along what would happen? Her anger boiled up inside her. 'You planned this deliberately, didn't you?' she accused, her tension mounting. 'When I refused to have dinner with you. And David . . .'

'I didn't plan for David to go and leave you unprotected, if that's what you mean,' Jago announced in a hard voice. 'But since he has, I didn't see any reason why I shouldn't take advantage of the fact.'

'You're despicable!' Storm hissed furiously. 'Why are you doing this? Isn't it enough that you've taken the station from him?'

'Don't be a little fool,' Jago replied harshly. 'I haven't taken the station away from him, as you put it, and as far as you're concerned, the fact that you claim you're in love with David has no bearing at all upon my actions, unless it's to prove to you that you don't begin to understand the meaning of the word.'

As he spoke his arm tightened, propelling her inexorably backwards until she was leaning against him, her head inches from his shoulder.

'Relax,' he breathed mockingly in her ear. 'I'm not an exhibitionist, Storm—I don't need an audience! You look as though you're perching on the edge of a particularly sabre-toothed precipice.'

'Because you've got bony knees,' Storm protested untruthfully.

She was unnerved by his soft laughter, stirring her hair.

'In that case sit a bit farther backwards,' he suggested. 'I've no objection to feeling your body against mine— unless it's the restrictive presence of our clothes and your friends.'

For a moment she was too shaken to speak. An inner tension seemed to be building up inside her, making her immediately aware of everything about him, conscious of his body with every shocked nerve ending.

Beneath the silky shirt she could see the beginnings of the dark tangle of hairs on his chest, and she was disturbingly aware of the warm male scent of his body. She had never felt like this with David!

She wetted her lips nervously, freezing as his hand curved possessively against her waist. She tried to wriggle away unobtrusively, but he refused to let her.

One by one the others started to leave. Pete was deep in conversation with the blonde girl he had been admiring earlier. Storm sighed under her breath. It looked as though Pete had completely forgotten her. She would have to phone her father and ask him to pick her up.

Jago shot back the cuff of his shirt and glanced at his watch. 'My antennae tell me that you're going to need a lift, Storm.'

'Not from you,' she replied dangerously.

His eyebrows rose. She could see the dark shadowing along his jaw where his beard grew. His eyes, she realised with a start, were two completely different shades of grey, the outer ring much darker than the inner.

'Frightened?' he asked dulcetly.

Storm summoned a brittle smile. 'No. I just wouldn't like to take you out of your way.'

His smile was mocking. 'You won't,' he promised, leaning forward to catch Pete's attention. 'I'll take Storm home,' he told the younger man crisply before she could protest. Any hopes Storm had had that Pete would take her himself died when she saw his face. Pete was far too engrossed in his blonde to worry about her!

'Ready?' Jago asked coolly.

Storm tried to control her inner tension. If only the pub was in walking distance of home—but it wasn't, and if she insisted on ringing her father Jago would know that he had broken through her guard.

In the car park Jago took her arm, directing her to a large, dark car, parked near the door. When he bent his head to unlock it, Storm realised that the car was not black as she had thought, but dark green and ominously familiar. It wasn't until they were both inside that she remembered from where.

'It was you!' she accused hotly. 'You were the madman who nearly drove me into the ditch the other morning!'

'If I had done it would have been your own fault,' Jago replied equably. 'You were driving on the wrong side of the road. Or had you forgotten?'

Storm stared mutinously out of the window. She wouldn't dignify the taunt with a response. But then another unnerving thought struck her. 'If this is your car, then you're the man who's bought the empty house next to ours.'

'Full marks for deduction,' he applauded lazily, without taking his eyes off the road.

Despite the luxurious comfort of her padded leather seat, Storm shivered with apprehension. To buy a house, Jago Marsh must be contemplating a lengthy stay in

Wyechester. But David had told her that he was merely joining them in an advisory capacity, for three months!

Jago flicked a switch and the relaxing strains of Country and Western music filled the car. Storm could not relax, though, her muscles were bunched in mute protest, aching as she fought against the trembling that had begun the moment they left the pub. The moment Jago brought the powerful car to a halt outside her parents' house she was reaching for the door handle.

Jago's hand closed over hers with petrifying swiftness, his face disturbingly close. Storm froze, panic coursing through her body. She could feel the hardness of his arm against her breasts and knew from the way he had tensed that he had guessed she was wearing nothing beneath the silk blouse.

His cool voice broke through her panic. 'You've locked the door—an accident, I take it?'

Unlike her he seemed in complete control of the situation. He pressed a button and pushed the door open.

Storm scrambled out with undignified haste, her mouth going dry with fear when Jago's lean form uncoiled itself from the driver's seat. All at once she experienced the most ridiculous sensation of anticlimax.

As though he guessed what she was feeling, Jago took her arm. 'Disappointed?' he drawled infuriatingly, his lips teasing a tendril of her hair as his hands slid down to hold her hips. Reaction shuddered through her, but she fought not to betray it, saying lightly;

'Why should I be?'

'Oh, no reason. I just got the impression that you were waiting for something. Like this, perhaps.'

He feathered a kiss across her cheek, teasing her lips slightly with a moist tongue before releasing her to say quietly. 'Well?'

'I can't think of anything I'd like less,' Storm told him acidly.

'No?' Iron-hard fingers gripped her chin, an unresisting wall of solid muscle meeting her trembling fingers. 'I don't make love in cars, Storm. I'm too old for that sort of adolescent escapade now. I prefer privacy and comfort for my lovemaking . . .'

It was uncanny how he managed to send her nervous system into chaos with nothing more than a handful of words.

'I don't care what you prefer, Jago,' she told him coldly. 'And you'll never get the opportunity to make love to me!'

'Is that so? Be careful, Storm. Some men might take that as an implicit invitation to prove to you just how wrong you are.'

A light went on in her parents' bedroom and to Storm's relief Jago stepped back, raising his hand in a brief salute before he strode round to the driver's door and slid into the car. The powerful engine made hardly any noise at all as it moved away, and Storm did not stop to watch him go.

Only later, when she was lying in bed, sleep evading her, did she give way to frightened tears. She felt like some small animal faced with a trap which was slowly but inexorably closing on her.

CHAPTER FOUR

To Storm's dismay she was nearly late for Jago's meeting, and this time through no fault of her own.

Her mother's Mini, obviously remembering Storm's less than respectful treatment the last time she had driven it, completely refused to start, and Mr Templeton had had to make a detour to drop Storm off.

She hurried into the office in Sue's wake just in time to hear the other girl saying apologetically that David had phoned from Oxford to say he had decided to stay on with his friends for a few days and would not be back until later in the week.

Jago received this news in silence, his eyes resting fleetingly on Storm's face as she stared at Sue.

'Did David ask for me?' she asked the other girl, sitting down next to Pete. Sue shook her head.

David hadn't been in touch with her at all over the weekend, and Storm wondered why not. They had never been the sort of couple who lived in one another's pockets, but all the same she had expected him to phone her at the very least.

'Any ideas what David's up to?' Pete whispered while Jago's attention was elsewhere.

Storm shook her head. 'Why should he be "up to" anything?' she whispered back. 'You know David. He's as straight as a die.'

'Oh yeah?' Pete drawled, but before she could take him up on the comment, Jago was enquiring coldly;

'Have you two quite finished?'

On her lap lay the folder containing her financial projections and her outlines for several publicity schemes she

wanted to put forward. She had spent all weekend working on the projects, painstakingly typing out columns of
figures, and she was forced to admit that the situation was
even worse than she had envisaged. If Mr Beton cancelled
his commercial—as he had threatened—it would be cata-
strophic. She sighed and tried to marshal her thoughts.

Jago was getting up. Today he was wearing an
immaculate navy suit, looking every inch the invincible
businessman, his eyes glittering over her as though he was
aware of the response she fought hard to control. What
was the matter with her? she asked herself in dismay as
awareness flooded through her, but she already knew.
Hard though she had tried to deny the truth, she could
not deny her response to Jago's dynamic sexual mag-
netism. The knowledge shocked and frightened her,
making her hands tremble as she straightened her papers.

'Right, if everyone's ready?'

No one dissented. Jago glanced round the room, then
leaned forward, resting his palms on top of the desk.

As far as Storm could see he had not prepared any
notes—certainly he wasn't reading from anything, but the
verbal castigation he gave them came with all the de-
cimating impact of a hail of machinegun fire.

His criticisms were not biased against any particular
member of the staff—Storm had to give him that, and he
was scrupulous in avoiding any reference to David's part
in their present plight. Again this was something she had
not expected, but instead of relieving her, it sent further
frissons of dismay along her already taut nerves. Somehow
or other she had imagined Jago would make use of David's
absence to turn him into a scapegoat, and if the truth
were known had been girding herself to leap to David's
defence. Now he had robbed her of the protection that
defence would have brought. Dragging her eyes from his
face, she forced herself to examine his criticisms. They
were valid, she was forced to admit, listening to him tick-

ing off on long fingers a list of faults and shortcomings, all the more effective for being delivered in that dry, telling voice.

Lack of enthusiasm, lack of initiative, lack of co-ordination between the various departments, no apparent attempt to get out and get the station noticed; the list was endless.

They were all culpable, Storm thought guiltily. His speech had opened her eyes to areas of deficiency she had hitherto been completely unaware existed.

When he had finished he looked at them.

'Right, I've had my say—now it's your turn. When I called this meeting I told you we would be fighting on opposite sides. Now it's up to you to convince me that in future I'm not going to have to wage war single-handed. We're all in this together—a team working for one ultimate goal—the success of this station, and if we all bear that in mind we'll get along fine.'

'As long as we remember who's the boss,' Storm muttered, goaded into the comment by his expression.

'Are you saying that you'd like to volunteer?' he asked softly. 'It's tough at the top, as they say, and something tells me you haven't got the sticking power.'

'Because I'm a woman, *Mr* Marsh?' Storm countered, trembling under his look. Whatever else happened he mustn't become aware of this ability he possessed to fire her senses into awareness of his masculinity.

She was subjected to an instant and thorough inspection that missed nothing, from her flushed cheeks right down to the clinging fit of her pale green jersey dress.

'Forgive me if I'm wrong,' Jago drawled, 'but I thought we were discussing the success, or lack of it, or Radio Wychester—not the women's movement.'

She wanted to say that being a woman had nothing to do with it—but she knew that this was not true. It had everything to do with it, and was the cause of the burning

resentment she experienced whenever he looked at her, as
though . . . as though she were his for the taking whenever
he chose, she thought bitterly.

'Anyone else got anything more to say? Something a
little more constructive this time,' he added with a dry
glance at Storm.

His invitation broke the ice. The complaints came
thicker than snow in a blizzard. The technicians started
the ball rolling. Jago listened in silence as they described
the under-capitalised state of their equipment.

'The entire venture was under-capitalised right from
the start,' he agreed, as he made a brief note on his pad.
'But something is going to be done about that,' he told
them crisply. 'Any other comments?'

One by one the others started to voice their opinions,
only herself remaining silent, Storm observed unhappily
as she listened to Jago questioning Pete.

'We'd thought of various schemes for boosting our
audience ratings,' the younger man was saying eagerly in
response to Jago's question. 'We did wonder about promoting a weekly disco and . . .'

'We?' Jago interrupted queryingly.

'Well, the idea was originally Storm's,' Pete admitted.
'She thought it would help to get the D.J.s known to the
public, but David wasn't too keen on the idea. In fact he
put a real damper on most of your ideas, didn't he,
Storm?' Pete asked her.

Storm refused to look at Jago.

'I expect he had his reasons,' she said noncommittally.

'Oh, come on,' Pete urged. 'What about the Samaritans
scheme you wanted to run, and the . . .'

'I'm sure Mr Marsh doesn't want to hear all about my
harebrained schemes,' Storm began lightly, but it was no
use. Jago was watching her carefully, his eyes narrowed.

'On the contrary,' he told her softly, 'I'm interested in
anything that would prove just one of you really wanted

to make a go of this venture.'

His sarcasm provoked Storm beyond caution. Pushing aside her advertising figures, she turned to face Jago.

'I did think we might launch a Samaritans-type scheme,' she admitted. 'The other, large stations do it. I feel, and have felt for a long time, that we need to improve our scope—extend our audience. The first thing I'm asked when I try to sell advertising is how is it going to improve the clients' sales. At the moment our audience is strictly limited . . .'

'An obstacle that other radio stations seem to have overcome,' Jago pointed out, obviously not intending to make things easy for her. For some reason his very opposition merely served to spur Storm on. She had a captive audience and the theme was very close to her heart. David was forgotten in her enthusiasm to prove that they could make a go of the station, and her eyes sparkled with conviction as she spoke.

'Involvement is the key,' she told him 'We need things like the Samaritans scheme—an open line for listeners to use to discuss their problems and get help. It would have to be confidential, of course, and we might even need to bring in a team of experts, doctors, lawyers and so on, who could be persuaded to give their time and knowledge to help the community.' She faltered a little, remembering how David had reacted to her idea. 'Too expensive, and too risky' had been how he had described it.

'Sounds okay,' Jago murmured noncommittally. 'What would you call it?'

She was a little taken aback. She had expected him to reject her idea out of hand. David had frequently told her that such a scheme was economically unviable, but she had countered by pointing out that it would give them invaluable publicity and be a declaration of their intention of participating fully in the life of the community.

'Call it?' She tried to collect her thoughts. 'Oh, I don't

know—Communicare, but David . . .'

'Didn't like it?' Jago asked with a wry smile. 'No, he wouldn't. A shallow water man is our David, which was why I was so surprised to find he had you,' he added in a voice that only Storm could hear. 'You're a deep water girl, Storm. An all or nothing girl.' His eyes held her captive. 'Right now you might have opted for nothing, but I intend to change all that. Now,' he added, addressing them all, 'any other ideas?'

'Storm has loads,' Pete said eagerly. 'There was that talent spotting competition you thought of, Storm, with the weekly disco, and the job-finder scheme, and the phone-in line for lonely housewives, the "adopt a granny" thing and . . .'

'Quite a girl for ideas, aren't you?' Jago asked with a sideways look. 'You've been doing your homework well too. These are all ideas used by the top local radio stations. There are others, of course. Wyechester has a large orphanage. How about launching an appeal to raise money for needy children? With Christmas coming up it should have instant appeal.'

'Great!' Pete enthused. 'We could have a special kids' slot on the Saturday morning show.'

'And we could use the outside broadcasting unit to ask children what they hope to get from Father Christmas— use their answers to underline the difference between the haves and the have-nots,' Storm added.

Jago returned to his chair.

'Now I know that you've got the ideas, why haven't they been put into practice? Well, Storm?'

He had tricked her, she thought despairingly. Her enthusiasm had betrayed her, or rather it had betrayed David, who had always been cautious about new ventures, but wild horses would not drag such an admission from her in front of Jago Marsh.

He was looking directly at her, but she avoided his

eyes, staring at the floor. The others weren't so discreet.

'David always said there wasn't enough money for anything but the basic services,' Pete grumbled.

'Well, from now on there will be,' Jago promised, leaving Storm to wonder resentfully where it was coming from. Did he have his own private mint? 'All the ideas you've put forward are excellent in their own way,' he told them. 'You left out promoting local sport, and group activities, but what we're really talking about here is commitment and caring. And these must be our guide lines from now on. For us to be a hundred per cent successful, we need to be a hundred per cent committed to the community—that's the secret of success. Now I don't want to overload your digestions. Go away and mull over what we've said this morning. We'll get together later in the week and decide where to start. Storm . . .'

She had been closing her file preparatory to leaving, but she lifted her head, watching him warily. If only David had been here to defend himself—but David was somewhere in Oxford. The thought made her heart ache, although she did not know why. Nor did she understand why she should feel as though David had let her down and left her unprotected to face Jago Marsh.

If Jago was aware of the reason for her hesitancy he ignored it, getting up to come and stand next to her.

'I've had a letter from John Harmer,' he told her unexpectedly. 'It seems he's been having second thoughts about that advertising campaign you were trying to sell him. He wants to see you.'

Storm could scarcely believe it. Her eyes lit up, her expression quite unguarded for once as she stared up at Jago.

'I'll go and phone him right now,' she began, but Jago shook his head.

'No need,' he told her. 'It's all been taken care of. We're both going out there this afternoon. I just wanted to warn you so that you could prepare yourself. I want to be in on this meeting.'

Didn't he trust her? Storm fumed later in her own office, while she rifled through the Harmer file. Or did he suspect that she wasn't up to securing the account? Either way it was scarcely flattering, and it was in a mood of reckless defiance that she prepared for the coming interview.

During the lunch break—which Storm elected to take at her desk so that Jago could not accuse her of neglecting any aspect of Mr Harmer's business—the phone rang. It was David, apologising for not being in touch with her before. 'When are you coming back?' she asked him, but he was evasive, his voice low and hard to hear as though he did not want to be overheard.

'Don't you want to hear about the meeting?' she asked him, puzzled by his restraint.

'The meeting? Oh, yes. How *did* it go?'

But Storm had the impression that he was not really interested, and she was just about to ask him if something was wrong when he said that he had to go and hurriedly rang off.

'Business or pleasure?' Jago asked, coming into the room as she replaced the receiver.

'It was David,' she told him shortly.

'Then it must have been business,' he mocked succinctly. 'I don't think David knows the first thing about pleasure.' His fingers lifted to her cheek, tucking a stray lock of hair behind her ear before she could prevent him, his eyes laughing at her flushed confusion. 'Neither do you, do you, Storm?' he asked softly. 'But I shall soon teach you.'

'What do you want?' she asked him coldly, dismayed by feelings his touch had aroused, and further disturbed when his eyebrows rose and he asked sardonically:

'Do you really need to ask me that? I thought I'd made

it perfectly obvious.' When she refused to retaliate he laughed again. 'Ah, you're beginning to learn. I came to see if you were ready to leave.'

'Leave?' Storm glanced at her watch. 'But you said the appointment was for three o'clock.'

'That's right,' he agreed urbanely, 'but I thought we'd have lunch first. No argument,' he said, forestalling her, and handed her her coat, making it obvious that he intended to hold it while she put it on. As she slid her arms reluctantly into it, she felt his hand lifting her hair from her neck and the light caress of his fingers against her nape was like an electric current jerking through her.

What was the matter with her? she asked herself nervously, picking up her folder and bag. She was reacting like a teenager on her first date. He had only touched her, for heavens sake. That was exactly the trouble, she admitted wryly. For some reason he only needed to touch her. She hoped to God he never discovered how susceptible she was to him. But there was no reason why he should as long as she kept her cool and didn't allow him to panic her into anything she could not get out of.

'Blushing?' he asked dulcetly as they stepped out into the crisp autumn afternoon. 'I didn't know girls still could.'

'It's the wind,' Storm prevaricated—obviously quite ineffectually, if the look he gave her as he unlocked the car was anything to go by.

Wyechester was not without its own very individual appeal, and today as they drove through the narrow streets, Storm was seeing it with fresh eyes. One or two Tudor buildings lingered on, rubbing shoulders with their more grandiose Georgian brethren. What was now the Town Hall and Council Offices had once been the local manor house and its gardens had been preserved for the use of the public. A modern health centre and library complex had been erected to the rear of the Queen Anne house, in such a manner that they did not detract from the charm of the original building.

Jago's car was as luxuriously impressive from the inside as it was from the outside. Storm had never travelled in such an expensive vehicle before, if one did not count the lift he had given her the other evening, and then she had been too preoccupied with other matters to pay much attention to her surroundings. Now as she forced herself to relax she examined the interior of the Ferrari, noticing the plushy comfort of the leather seat and the unobtrusive signs of luxury all round her.

Pete's voice floated out of the stereo radio—she had forgotten it was his turn to D.J. the lunch-time pop session, and she lay back, closing her eyes and listening to the music.

'Calder's got the right touch,' Jago commented, leaning forward to adjust the volume slightly, 'and he's ambitious—he should go far. What did David want?'

The question caught her off guard, bringing her upright, two spots of colour burning in her cheeks.

'Nothing that has anything to do with you,' she said with brittle emphasis, unprepared for the speed with which he stopped the car, swearing savagely as he pulled off the road and turned to face her.

'Don't try to tell me he rang up to whisper sweet nothings to you,' he said savagely, 'because I just won't believe you. Winters hasn't got the slightest conception of what it takes to turn a woman like you on, has he, Storm?' In fact I'm willing to bet that's something no man has ever done.'

There was a strange, tight pain deep inside her, as though Jago was invading the deepest recesses of her privacy, bringing to the light of day things she'd thought safely hidden from everyone, including herself.

'Don't be ridiculous,' she began, but his hands cupped her face, his thumbs caressing her skin with a sensual expertise that sent shivers of awareness coursing through her.

'Don't lie to me, Storm,' he murmured. 'I was right wasn't I? No man has ever aroused you, least of all David.'

'I'm not frigid, if that's what you're trying to say,' Storm prevaricated, trembling under the intensity of his regard. They were on a deserted stretch of country road, and she was aware of him in a way that she had never been aware of anyone before. It wasn't just him she feared, she acknowledged with painful honesty, it was herself as well. She might despise him. She might not want the desire he said he felt for her, but she *was* pulsatingly aware of it.

'No? Then let's prove it, shall we?' he drawled, his arms going round her, holding her captive as his lips feathered a teasing caress against hers.

She wanted to run and yet she wanted to stay. She was completely powerless to withstand his practised arousal, his slow, determined assault upon her senses, and the kisses that took her far, far beyond anything she'd known with anyone else.

'Definitely not frigid,' Jago agreed, lifting his mouth from hers. 'But inexperienced, and holding back . . .'

'Of course I'm holding back, as you put it,' Storm said shakily, trying to fight against what he was doing to her. 'I'm in love with David, or have you forgotten?'

'Hadn't you?' Jago asked succinctly, his hand closing over hers as she reached frantically for the door handle. 'I've locked it,' he told her dryly when she turned a panic-stricken face towards him. 'This is the last time you fling David Winters in my face, Storm. Before I've finished with you, you're going to forget he ever existed.'

'Let me out of here!' she sobbed, her fists pounding the inflexible wall of his chest, but he caught her hands with expert ease, his eyes smoky grey as he sneered coldly:

'Your first mistake, Storm. Never start a fight on the opposition's home ground.'

'Fight?' She stared at him in incredulity. 'I don't want to fight . . .'

'Oh, but you do,' he said softly, 'otherwise you'd never have reminded me of David. Or was it yourself you were trying to remind? Was that it, Storm? Were you holding David up in front of you like a shield?'

He was far too close to the truth, Storm admitted shakily.

'I love David,' she reiterated childishly, and was instantly punished for her folly as his mouth closed over hers, his hands exploring her body with ruthless economy, shattering all her preconceived ideas of how she would react in such circumstances, as he moulded her hips against the hardness of his thighs, and then slid his hands upwards, cupping her breasts, his fingers probing the soft flesh as he murmured unkindly, 'No bra? Now why was that, I wonder? Were you hoping for something like this?'

She went rigid, her eyes flaming with anger.

'How dare you!' she hissed. 'I loathe having you touch me. You make me sick, you . . .'

Her words were cut short, as his mouth ground her lips back against her teeth until her breath seemed trapped inside her lungs, the angry raking of her fingernails against his shoulders ignored, as his mouth moved down over her throat, leaving her powerless to stop his unhurried invasion of her senses, the explosive feel of his mouth on her skin, awakening her to raw desire. She gasped, shuddering as his teeth tugged at the buttons on her blouse, his lips suddenly persuasive as they caressed her breast.

Heat flooded through her. No one had ever touched her like this before, and she had never imagined that she could feel this . . . this . . . She moaned, unable to deny her arousal, pressing instinctively against him as his mouth

moved against her skin, his tongue circling her nipple, the
tormenting caress starting an ache deep inside her that
obliterated all rational thought. She was beyond reason,
beyond anything but what his hands and mouth were
doing to her, and when his mouth returned to hers her
lips parted for him on a husky groan, allowing him whatever licence he desired. She was lying underneath him,
his thighs like steel where they crushed her down into the
supple leather, but she didn't care.

Only when Jago tugged impatiently at his tie, un-
fastening his shirt so that she could feel the harshness of
his body hair against her breasts, did Storm realise what
was happening. She struggled to sit up, pushing ineffectually at his chest, shaking with guilt and terror. How
could she have allowed him to touch her like that, to . . .
She shuddered, closing her eyes and trying to pull her
blouse round her.

'Can David make you feel like that?' Jago asked com-
prehensively. 'And don't tell me you didn't feel a thing,
Storm, or I might be tempted to show you how easy it
would be to blot David Winters from your mind for ever.'

'No!' Storm mumbled, shivering with despair. Even
now she couldn't believe what had happened. Pride made
her say angrily, 'And I do love David, I don't care what
you say. I know you can arouse me,' she admitted bitterly.
'You've proved that. I hope to God it gives you some
satisfaction, because it doesn't give me any. I loathe you,
Jago,' she said quietly, 'and now I loathe myself as well.'

'You loathe me?' Jago said derisively. 'You've got a
damned funny way of showing it. You wanted me, Storm,
whatever you say to the contrary, and you know it. But
still you cling to this "love" you claim to have for David.
Why?' he asked softly.

Storm didn't reply. With shaking fingers she fastened
her blouse, dismayed by the feeling that flooded through
her as she remembered the feel of his mouth against her

skin, a deep yearning ache throbbing through her.

What would he say if she told him she clung to David because she was frightened of what he was doing to her? Run a mile, probably, she thought derisively. Jago had no compunction about arousing her body, but he wouldn't want any emotional involvement. Perhaps she ought to tell him, she thought wryly. But she couldn't. She couldn't reveal her deep fear of such a commitment to him, not after the way he had just breached her defences.

'No answer?' he prompted. 'Very wise. I meant what I said about obliterating David from your mind, Storm, and every time you mention him and love in the same breath I shall remind you of how very easy it is for me to do what he finds impossible.'

Her face flamed. She couldn't help it. She longed to deny that he had aroused her, or to tell him that she and David were lovers, but she sensed that to do either would provoke another ruthlessly enforced example of what he could do to her. And if she had doubted him before she did so no longer. He had the power to make her feel desire. But desire was not love, she reminded herself, and mere sexual appeasement no part of what she wanted from life.

'I should imagine it's possible for any experienced male to get some sort of reaction from a woman, especially when she's . . .'

'Got less knowledge about the opposite sex than it would take to cover a postage stamp?' Jago jeered. 'Sure— it's possible.'

After that, mercifully, he turned away from her, starting the engine, leaving her to cope with her disturbed senses alone.

Why did he have the power to make her feel like this? she asked herself bitterly, trying to concentrate on the scenery, but all that she could think of was her own betraying response to his calculated assault upon her senses, her face flaming anew as she remembered her abandoned reaction.

'Aren't we stopping for lunch?' she asked him awkwardly, trying to dispel the memory.

Jago glanced at the clock on the dashboard and shook his head. 'Our slight altercation seems to have affected my appetite—for food at least. Why, are you hungry?'

'Not particularly.'

She refused to look at him. In point of fact she had never felt less like food. Her stomach was churning with all the efficiency of a high speed electric mixer, and to much the same effect. The thought of food was totally nauseating. It came to her on a wave of dismay that she wanted nothing quite so much as the peace and quiet of her own room so that she could indulge in a good cry, which was most unlike her—in fact she could not remember when she had last cried, and it certainly hadn't been over a man!

Jago on the other hand had never looked more self-possessed. Storm watched him out of the corner of her eye, noticing small hitherto unimportant things about him, such as the way his lean fingers held the steering wheel, the powerful thrust of his thigh muscles whenever he changed gear. Hastily she averted her eyes, forcing herself to relax.

After all that had happened, she thought shakily, he obviously still expected her to go on to this meeting and behave as though nothing out of the ordinary had occurred. What was he, a man or a machine?

Her shaking legs told her the answer, although she did not want to acknowledge the message they were relaying to her—Jago Marsh was very much a man, as her aching body knew to its cost.

Their destination, Harmer Brothers' Mill, was on the outskirts of a small village, tucked away in a corner of the Cotswolds, an enviable location, and one which Storm usually enjoyed visiting. Today she was too strung up to pay much attention to the familiar landscape. At her side she caught Jago's eye as he glanced out of the car window. His dark hair lay smooth and sleek against his skull and she fought to drag her eyes away, remembering how less than an hour before she had...She must forget that it had ever happened, she told herself. Everyone was entitled to one mistake, and she had now made hers, and yet her body continued to quiver restlessly.

The Harmers had adapted an old watermill for their needs; the cream Cotswold stone of the original building blending perfectly with its surroundings. The mill wheel had been lovingly restored, and Storm reflected that the tranquillity of the double-storey building set next to the sheet of placid water would be difficult to rival anywhere.

Inside it was a very different story, and John Harmer was every inch the businessman as he strode out of his office to greet them.

Storm had expected the two men to conduct the interview over her head, but she was pleasantly surprised, when they entered John Harmer's office, to be introduced to a friendly-looking young man of her own age.

'My son Greg,' John Harmer explained with fatherly pride. 'He's working for his Ph.D. at the moment, but occasionally he spares us a few hours here and there.' He shook his head, looking at his son. 'I had hoped he would be taking over from me long before now.'

Greg Harmer laughed, his pleasant brown eyes crinkling with amusement. 'Come off it, Dad, you're a long way off retirement yet—if ever. You know this mill's your pride and joy.'

'With good reason,' Jago agreed. 'I notice you stick as closely to traditional tweeds as possible.'

Storm gave Jago full marks for doing his homework, as John Harmer acknowledged his comment.

'Mm. We do use modern dyes, though. Nowadays people want a wider, more subtle range of colours, but we do try to be as authentic as possible. We sell a lot of stuff abroad, of course, especially France and America. In fact our overseas sales greatly exceed whatever we market here. Our product isn't cheap and quite frankly, there isn't the demand for it.' He looked at Storm. 'That's one of the reasons why I wasn't very enthusiastic when you came to see me.'

Storm winced as she remembered his acerbic remarks about not being a philanthropist, acutely aware of Jago's powerful muscled body towering over her.

'We're very grateful to be given a second chance of convincing you that advertising on Radio Wyechester will be worthwhile, Mr Harmer,' she replied politely.

'Don't thank me. Greg's the one who suggested I should think again. I was telling him about some of your suggestions...'

'Yes,' Greg Harmer interrupted eagerly, 'I particularly liked the idea of using a Fenella Fielding type voice-over to put across the sophisticated aspect of our cloth, especially with the humorous undertones you suggested.'

Storm warmed to him. He was open and uncomplicated, and best of all he didn't intimidate and threaten her like Jago did.

'I'm only copying what's already been used—successfully,' she said deprecatingly, turning back to his father. 'I think there's a market for your cloth here, Mr Harmer,' she told the older man. 'You may not know it, but there are several small specialist manufacturers operating locally, who I'm sure would be very interested in your cloth, and there's also talk of a French concern starting up a factory complex near Bristol.'

John Harmer looked surprised and impressed.

'You've done your research pretty thoroughly, young lady,' he said. 'I only learned about the French the other week myself. So you think your radio station can help sell my cloth, do you?'

His tone was faintly paternal and a little condescending, but Storm refused to let it get to her. She was used to this attitude from older men, and took a pride in turning their indulgence to respect when one of her campaigns succeeded. However, she did not normally have Jago Marsh breathing down her neck, and it was hard to pretend that he wasn't there or that she wasn't affected by his presence, the tiny hairs on the nape of her neck prickling with awareness every time he moved.

Forcing herself to appear composed, she smiled at John Harmer.

'Yes, I do,' she told him firmly.

'And so do I,' Greg Harmer chimed in admiringly. 'You really know your stuff, don't you? And you're such a tiny little thing. How did you get into radio advertising?'

Smilingly Storm gave him a brief potted biography. His eyes widened a little as she mentioned the agency she had been with in Oxford, and he commented appreciatively, 'They're one of the most successful in the country, aren't they? You must have been very good to be taken on by them straight from college.'

In actual fact she had come first in a competition they had sponsored and her prize had been a job with the agency, but Storm only smiled and said that she expected she had just been lucky. She wanted to steer the conversation away from personal channels and back to her campaign, but was a little taken aback when Jago suddenly cut in crisply, his eyes impatient.

'If you're agreeable Miss Templeton could draw up a commercial for your appraisal and then we'll run it for a month at a special rate—just to give you an idea of what can be achieved. At the end of that month we'll get together. I'm sure you'll be pleasantly surprised by the results.'

He spoke with such an air of calm authority that Storm wasn't surprised to see John Harmer waver. Encouraged by his son's enthusiasm, he eventually capitulated and gave his agreement to Jago's suggestion.

She should have felt elated, she thought as they drove away, for both John and Greg Harmer had seemed pleased with the results of their discussion, but instead she felt bone-weary, her head throbbing with a tension headache, and it was all she could do to force herself to appear calm as they headed back towards Wyechester.

She glanced at Jago once, shocked by the icy anger glittering in his eyes, and wondered what she had done wrong.

'You forgot about dear David back there fast enough, didn't you?' he gritted at her when they were on the open road. 'I thought I must be seeing things when you turned on the charm for young Harmer, *and* he fell for it. Is that how you get the advertising? No wonder it's so badly down,' he jeered contemptuously. 'You might come on with the promises, but that's all they are, isn't it?'

At first Storm was too shocked to speak. She stared at him in a daze, trying to see her behaviour through his eyes. She hadn't flirted with Greg; she had just been polite. She knew he had quite fancied her, of course; but that was all it had been.

'I think that's a despicable accusation!' she said at last, trembling with indignation. 'I don't understand you at all. First you tell me that you want me, and seem to expect me to fall into your arms, delirious with excitement at the thought of becoming your mistress, and then you act like a Victorian father because I smile at one of our clients!' Her voice was deliberately scathing. It had to be to conceal the fear she felt as she saw the anger leaping to life in his eyes.

'Delirious with excitement—there's a phrase to catch the imagination,' he said softly, his anger doused and another expression taking its place, causing Storm's blood to pound through her veins with slow sweetness. For a moment the dark lashes hid his expression from her, and then they swept up and she was caught in the steely glitter of his eyes as they moved slowly over her body in such a way that her clothes were as good as stripped from her, his mouth cruel as he surveyed her flushed cheeks and trembling mouth.

'And you were, weren't you, Storm?' he asked softly, his eyes deriding her. 'I could have taken you there and then and we both know it. Oh, don't worry,' he said with lazy confidence, stretching out a hand to touch the curve of her throat and stroking the skin lingeringly, 'I'm going to, but not until you admit that you don't give a damn for David and that you're only hiding behind the protection you think he can give you.'

The words released her from the spell of his touch. Shrinking back, she glared at him.

'Then you'll wait for ever!' she spat unwisely. 'Because I do love David.'

She didn't know which unnerved her more, his soft laugh or the way his eyes lingered mockingly on her face before dropping to where her breasts swelled softly against her blouse.

Damn him! she thought explosively, biting hard on her lip, trying to contain her reaction. She could almost feel her body responding to that look, but she refused to give him the satisfaction of knowing it, just as she refused to admit the truth of what he was saying. He would never hear her say that she didn't love David, she told herself savagely, drawing some comfort from the knowledge that she could deny him with her mind, even while her body surrendered.

To her surprise, when they reached the intersection which led to Storm's home, Jago turned left instead of taking the right fork for Wyechester.

'I'm taking you home,' he said briefly by way of explanation, his eyes mocking. 'You've had a big day, and you look all eyes. If you want to know the secret I'll tell you—try to remain dispassionate.'

She wasn't sure if his enigmatic remark was meant to apply to their meeting with the Harmers or what had happened earlier. Either way, she told herself, she didn't want to know, but she still said lightly, 'Something you're very good at, I'm sure. You'd never let your passions rule your head, would you?'

'Like to find out?' he asked urbanely. 'If so, it can be arranged.'

She gave him a scathing look, trying to match his own irony. 'I'm sure it can. But I happen to be choosy.'

For a moment something flared in his eyes and she wondered if she had pushed him too far, but then he smiled grimly, his eyes openly sardonic.

'Nice try,' he told her. 'But if David is an example of your taste, you wouldn't know where to begin.'

As he manoeuvred his car into her parents' drive, Storm saw her father in the front garden, tidying up the flower beds. He straightened up when he heard the car.

'Hello, you're early, Storm,' he greeted her. 'I was just about to ring up and see if you wanted a lift home.'

'*I'm* early,' Storm teased affectionately, resolutely ignoring Jago. 'What about you? Working part-time now, are we?'

'I'll thank you to show a little more respect for your aged parent,' Mr Templeton grumbled, smiling at Jago. 'No lectures this afternoon—one of the few perks of stuffing the heads of the young with information. Apart from that it's the labours of Hercules all over again.'

'Come off it,' Storm scoffed. 'You love every minute of it. All those dishy young girls!'

'Not a patch on your mother.' He turned to Jago, his hand outstretched. 'As Storm seems to have forgotten her manners, I'd better introduce myself. I'm Richard Templeton, and you must be Jago Marsh.' His eyes twinkled a little as they shook hands and he turned to smile at Storm. 'Looks perfectly normal to me.'

Storm knew her father was deliberately teasing her, but she still blushed infuriatingly. Her father was thanking Jago for bringing her home and he replied easily that it hadn't brought him out of his way.

'Jago has taken over Mr Simons' house, Dad,' Storm explained, wishing for some reason that it had not been necessary to introduce him to her father. The damage was done now, however.

Mr Templeton looked interested and said to Jago, 'So we're neighbours, then? We must get together some time.'

Storm knew from her father's tone that the invitation was genuinely meant and hid her surprise. Mr Templeton did not suffer fools gladly, and Storm had often been a little hurt at her father's casual dismissal of David, and she wondered a little resentfully how Jago had managed to win her father's respect on the strength of less than two minutes' conversation. Her father wouldn't be so ready to accept if he knew how Jago had treated *her*, she thought angrily, two spots of colour burning in her cheeks as she fought against the intrusive memory of how she had reacted to him. She had fallen into his hands like an over-ripe plum, she lashed herself, her colour spreading as she remembered her fevered reaction, and she marched past Jago, ignoring him as she turned to ask her father if he was coming.

Richard Templeton raised his eyebrows a little and Storm bit her lip, knowing that she was being silently reprimanded.

'You go on ahead,' he told her, and as she hurried away she heard Jago say, 'I'd better be on my way.'

'Pleasant chap,' her father commented later when they were having dinner. 'Still . . .' he glanced rather thoughtfully at his daughter, 'I don't think I'd recommend getting on the wrong side of him. My instincts tell me that he could be a tough nut to crack, eh, Storm?'

'Perhaps,' she agreed noncommittally, her eyes faintly hazy with a pain she wasn't ready to admit to, and she was thankful when the subject was dropped. Only now, away from Jago's disturbing presence, could she start to analyse her reactions to him, and yet for some reason she found herself reluctant to do so.

CHAPTER FIVE

THE telephone rang while Storm and her parents were watching television.

'I'll get it,' Mr Templeton told Storm, disappearing into the hall. A few moments later he reappeared.

'It's for you,' he told Storm. 'David.'

David! Her pulses leapt— but not with excitement, she acknowledged unhappily. What she was experiencing was guilt. For the first time it occurred to her to question David's feelings for her and wonder why he had never tried to put their relationship on a more intimate basis. The question had never bothered her before. David respected her, but now she wondered if it was respect or merely lack of desire that kept their romance so tepid.

His voice sounded a little strained, and Storm waited for him to tell her why he had elected to stay on in Oxford.

'Is something wrong, David?' she asked him when several minutes had gone by without an explanation. It wasn't like David to phone merely for a chat.

'You could say that,' he said abruptly. 'Storm, I'm leaving the station. I have no choice. Marsh has made it pretty plain that he means to take over, so I'm getting out while I can.'

'But, David, you can't do that! The station is you!' Storm protested, knowing even as she spoke that she was lying. The station was now indisputably Jago's.

'I've had an offer for my shares—not that I hold that many, and I've decided to take it up. I'm using the money to go into business with a friend of mine in Oxford. He owns a bookshop and I'm going in as his partner. Nothing as grand as being Controller of Radio Wyechester, but I doubt if Jago would have allowed me to retain that title much longer.'

There was self-pity in the words, but Storm barely took it in. She couldn't get over the fact that David had made these decisions without a word to her, and she felt as though a protective layer of skin had been ripped away from her, forcing her to see things she had previously ignored.

'If it's what you want, David,' she sighed. 'But what about us?'

'Us?' Was it her imagination or was the word guarded? 'It doesn't make any difference to us, Storm—unless you were more interested in my position than me.'

Unhappiness choked her for a second. 'That's a hateful thing to say!' she whispered. By rights she should be the one making the accusations, and she shivered a little with apprehension. She could have sworn she knew David inside out, and yet all at once she felt as though she did not know him at all.

'Why didn't you tell me?' she asked.

There was silence, then he replied defensively, 'I thought you might let it slip out before I'd got everything fixed up. I didn't want Marsh to know until I was sure myself.'

'When will you be back?' Storm asked him, her mind still trying to grapple with what he had told her. David running a bookshop! It would suit him, she acknowledged with a shock. She could just see him in shabby tweeds poring over some ancient volume.

'I don't know.' He sounded evasive. 'Don't do anything stupid yourself, Storm,' he warned her. 'When the news breaks Jago is going to look round for a scapegoat. He can say what he likes, but he needs me more than he thinks. He still doesn't know his way round the station, and he could waste one hell of a lot of time and money finding it.' He sounded as though the thought gave him a good deal of satisfaction.

'I tried to speak to you this afternoon,' he went on, 'but you were out.'

'We went to see Mr Harmer,' Storm told him mechanically. 'I think we've secured his advertising.'

There was a pause, and then David's voice, faintly metallic, over the wires, saying with false enthusiasm, 'Clever girl! I've got to go now. We'll get together when I get home.'

He hung up before she could ask him when he would be coming home, and she shivered as she replaced the receiver. She had never thought for one moment that David would give up the station without a fight. What pressure had Jago brought to bear on him to make him do so? Had he threatened to tell the I.B.A. that he didn't think David would ever make a go of it? Storm wouldn't put it past him. He was just the ruthless sort of bastard who would do something like that, she reflected. God, how she hated him! Her fists were clenched tight with the violence of her anger. He had said he would obliterate David from her mind. And from her life? She was letting her imagination run away with her, she told herself; Jago Marsh was not the sort of man to let mere desire for a woman colour his decisions. No, his desire to get rid of David had nothing to do with her.

'Something wrong?' Richard Templeton asked when Storm rejoined them. She was moving like a sleepwalker, her eyes dull and clouded.

'David's leaving the station,' she told her parents dully. 'Apparently it's all arranged. He's joining a friend in Oxford who owns a bookshop as a partner . . .'

'And never told you a word about it until it was a fait accompli?' Storm's father asked in thinly veiled irony. 'I think it's time you started asking yourself where you stand in David's life, Storm, and he in yours.'

'There were reasons,' Storm responded defensively. 'He

didn't want anyone at the station to know . . .'

'Anyone? Is that all you are to him?'

Storm felt faintly sick. Two days ago she would have denied the question without hesitation, but since then her life and emotions had been turned upside down, her eyes opened to things she had never noticed before.

'I don't know,' she admitted with pain. 'All I do know is that somehow Jago Marsh is responsible for David leaving, and I hate him for it,' she said childishly.

'Aren't you jumping to conclusions?' her father commented mildly. 'You know, love, loyalty is a good thing in its way, but sometimes it can be taken too far—it's called fanaticism,' he teased gently.

There was a tight ball of mingled tears and anger at the back of Storm's throat.

'Is that a kind way of telling me I'm a fanatic?' she asked.

Her father's eyes were gentle. 'No, I'm just reminding you that even the best of us can sometimes be guilty of closing our eyes to what we don't want to see. No one forced David to make the decision to leave—he did it of his own volition. Now I'm not saying that he might not have had some justification,' he added when Storm opened her mouth to protest, 'but I'm sure he isn't the martyr you seem to believe. Think, Storm, he's known for some time that Jago would be joining you, but he waits until now to make his decision. If you're honest with yourself you'll admit that it's more the action of a coward than a hero. David is no match for Jago Marsh and he knows it.'

'You've only met Jago once,' Storm retorted, stung into a fresh defence of David.

'My dear,' Mr Templeton said very dryly, 'everything about him proclaims the type of man he is. He won't suffer fools gladly. You have the right to think of David however you choose, Storm, but you must remember that you can't impose your views on others. They too are free to make their own choice. Think, child, you've always had a soft spot for a lame dog, and if you're honest you'll admit that it is exactly what David is and always will be. If you tie your life to his, he'll lean on you all through it. Are you strong enough to carry that sort of burden? Be honest with yourself, Storm, and don't let loyalty blind you to reality.'

'I suppose you think Jago Marsh would make a better husband,' Storm said recklessly, tears not far away. 'Well, if you do, it's you who are avoiding reality this time— Jago Marsh wouldn't even begin to understand the degree of commitment it takes to make a marriage!'

It was obvious to Storm the moment she walked into the office the next morning that the news of David's resignation had broken. Pete and Sue were so deep in conversation that they barely noticed her approach until Sue looked up. She flushed rather defensively and muttered something about seeing to the mail, leaving Storm alone with Pete.

'So old David's turned tail and run,' Pete commented unkindly. 'Can't say I'm surprised. Best thing all round, if you ask me.'

'Well, I didn't,' Storm said bitterly. 'And I don't know how you can say that, after all that David's done . . .'

'Oh yeah? Like drop a soggy wet blanket over everything we've ever come up with that might make the station a success. Sure I'm going to miss him like crazy,' he jeered callously. 'Sneaky too. I bet you didn't know what was going on, did you?'

His words were too close to the truth for comfort, and Storm flushed angrily.

'He didn't want to do anything before, because he thought that he and Jago Marsh could work together amicably,' she retorted stiffly.

Pete lifted his eyes to heaven. 'God help us,' he murmured piously. 'She actually believes it! How naïve can you get! Come down off your cloud, Storm. Face facts. David has handed in his resignation because the competition is just too stiff for him and that's the truth, only you're too damned stubborn to admit it.'

It was what her father had said, only put far less gently, but Storm ignored him, awareness suddenly prickling over her as a door opened in the corridor. She knew without looking round who it was. Dear Lord, she wondered helplessly, how had everything about him become so familiar to her in so short a space of time?

She turned in time to see Jago's eyes graze her skin, her grey jumper and lavender skirt no protection at all against those dissecting eyes. She gave a start when she realised that he wasn't alone. Sam Townley, their main backer, was with him, and Sam was looking far from pleased. No doubt Jago had been trying to force Sam to dig a little deeper into his pocket, Storm thought in grim satisfaction. He'd need a mechanical bulldozer to do that. Her smile faded as she saw the girl emerging from the office behind the two men: Angie Townley. Storm's mouth compressed. She didn't like the supermarket baron's daughter. Angie had a flat in London and a job which she vaguely described as freelance modelling. She was exactly Jago's type, Storm reflected, watching the way the blonde girl draped herself beside his lean body, her mouth pouting provocatively, as her eyes slid warningly over Storm.

The trembling awareness she had felt deep in the pit of her stomach the moment she saw Jago increased as he walked towards her, Angie's eyes spitting fire.

'Waiting for something, Storm?' he drawled as she stood rooted to the spot.

The awareness fled, replaced by red-hot anger. 'Yes,' she told him through gritted teeth, 'I wanted to have a word with you, *Mr* Marsh.'

His eyes narrowed at her challenging tone, but there was no other acknowledgement to show that he had seen her anger. He pushed back his cuff and glanced impatiently at his watch, and the action inflamed Storm's smouldering temper.

'Don't worry—what I have to say to you won't delay you for your lunch appointment,' she told him pointedly, staring through Angie.

'No,' Jago agreed coldly, 'it won't. Pete,' he instructed the D.J., 'give Angie and Mr Townley an inspection of the studios, will you. I won't be very long,' he told them as Pete hurried forward. He closed the door to his office and turned to face Storm, his eyes like splinters of ice. 'Don't you ever talk to me in front of anyone else like that again,' he warned her.

'But it's okay for me to do it in private?' Storm lashed back. 'Some chance!'

'Come off it, Storm.' His change of mood caught her off guard. 'I know you're not indifferent to me, but you've made your token gesture for the day, so what do you want?'

'David phoned me,' she began, refusing to be put off by his steely inspection.

'To cry on your shoulder?'

Something seemed to shiver between them, making the atmosphere in the small room dangerously explosive, and Storm lashed out at him, trying to destroy whatever it was that triggered off the emotion she could almost taste, but Jago caught her wrist in an inflexible grip, forcing her arm back, until she was biting her lip to prevent herself from crying out loud.

'Oh no, you don't, my beauty,' he warned her softly. 'I'm not your precious David, Storm Templeton. You hurt me and I hurt you right back—and on this occasion the muscle's all on my side.'

'And don't you just love it!' Storm flashed at him. She must be crazy doing this, she thought numbly as she saw the anger leaping to life and knowing it was too late to contain it. The violence of her own response to it shocked her, freezing the hot words clamouring for utterance. She was used to her own quickly flaring temper, the sudden spurt of rage followed by the equally sudden calm, but never before had she ever been moved to such intense fury—never had she actually wanted to strike someone and physically hurt them—yes, actually inflict pain—as she had wanted to do to Jago Marsh. Her lack of self-control was humiliating and her hands clenched into small mute fists.

'Heaven knows I've done my best to be patient with you, Storm,' Jago said savagely. 'You really believe in trying your luck, don't you? Or is it just blind trust—like that blind "love" you claim to have for David? You think I've got more control of my temper than you have of yours, is that it?'

As though his words had triggered off an automatic response Storm responded heatedly, 'I do love David. I do love him.'

'Like hell you do,' Jago returned flatly. 'Now I've got just five minutes, so tell me what you wanted.'

'It's David,' Storm whispered. 'As if you didn't know. How could you do this to him? How could you force him to leave the station he's built up from nothing? Don't you care that you've stripped his pride to the bone and made him look nothing in the eyes of everyone else? Or does that kind of thing give you some sort of kick?'

She had made him angry—very angry, but nothing would make her back down. In some odd way the mounting tension within the confining walls of the small office stimulated rather than frightened her. Jago's immobile stance challenged and she rose to the implicit challenge, her breath coming jerkily between her lips as his eyes slitted, their smouldering heat grazing her skin, his jaw taut where a muscle beat sporadically against the tanned skin.

'Finished?' Quiet though his voice was it stopped Storm in her tracks. 'Good,' he said softly as she licked dry lips. 'Now it's my turn to indulge in a few home truths. You see yourself as David's champion, don't you, Storm, righting the wrongs imposed by a cruel oppressor— namely myself. Has it never occurred to you that you're usurping *his* role? God, you're incredible!' he told her. 'How you can sit there and accuse me of humiliating him I just don't know. What the hell do you think you're doing to him? You haven't just humiliated the guy, you've damned near emasculated him as well!'

Storm went paper-white, clutching at the desk for support.

'No!' she moaned protestingly. 'It isn't like that . . .'

'Of course it's like that,' Jago said softly. 'Now I know he's never made it with you, and he never will, will he, Storm? Do you enjoy turning him into a sexless pet dog— does that turn you on? What the hell are you, Storm, or daren't you put a name to it?'

'It's not true! I'm not like that!' She ached with a pain that could not be ignored, her heart beating feverishly against her ribs. She felt as though she'd been ripped apart and was slowly bleeding to death with Jago watching her, his cold grey eyes following every betraying gesture.

'Stop looking at me like that,' she stammered, covering her face with her hands. 'I'm not like that!'

'Aren't you?' Jago pressed savagely, tearing her hands away from her eyes and forcing her to meet the sardonic coldness of his. 'Prove it to me, then, Storm. Give me one instance of when you've let pure instinct dictate your actions. Give me one example of when you've been a woman first!'

Sickness clawed at the pit of her stomach. There was only one occasion, and he shouldn't need reminding of it. A shudder began somewhere deep inside her, pain spreading slowly through her, every instinct warning her to escape. This man was dangerous. He had torn her with the savagery of his words and now he meant to destroy her pride and leave her bleeding at his feet.

She looked up at him with blank eyes, backing away from him towards the door, but it was too late. His shadow fell between her and the door. She knew he had seen her instinctive withdrawal, and his lips tightened, twisting sarcastically.

'Look at me, Storm,' he commanded softly.

She looked down at the floor. If he saw her eyes he would know what he had done to her. When she felt his fingers on her chin, she closed them, gritting her teeth, as they caressed her throat and the smooth hollows behind her ears.

She felt his breath graze her skin. 'Open your eyes, Storm. I want you to look at me.'

Panic coursed through her. She shivered and knew he had felt her reaction. 'Now what have I said to provoke this reaction?' Jago mused thoughtfully above her, his hands sliding over her back, propelling her against him. 'Whatever it was, it hurt, didn't it, Storm?'

'There's no way you could hurt me,' she denied breathlessly, opening her eyes.

He was looking straight at her, his eyes lazily amused. 'Is that so? I should have thought there were any number of ways,' he said quietly, his hands tightening meaningfully over her slight frame. 'At a guess I'd say you'd never had a lover, Storm,' he added thoughtfully. 'Poor David, I'll bet he doesn't have the faintest idea about what you're keeping hidden under all that ice.'

'I thought you just said I couldn't be a woman,' Storm countered unwisely, wriggling away from the sensuous movement of his hands over her hips.

'Not that you couldn't, just that you hadn't. But you will,' he promised softly without taking his eyes from her trembling lips.

Storm wanted to deny his words, but she could not, just as she could not prevent her lips from parting as his mouth covered them. At their touch piercing sweetness flowed through her, turning her blood to molten fire.

'I don't believe David's even kissed you properly,' Jago murmured huskily against her mouth. 'Put your arms round me, Storm,' he whispered. 'I want to feel you against me.'

Even the words were subtly designed to undermine her willpower she thought despairingly as her body quivered and against her will her arms circled his neck, her fingers drawn to the thick night darkness of his hair.

His arms held her against him and her flesh seemed to melt from her bones, a feeling that she knew must be desire beating up over her, her mouth parting mindlessly under the domination he was exerting.

It was like drowning, Storm thought hazily; like being caught on a huge rolling wave and subjected to its will, only sooner or later the wave would fling her back down on to the beach exhausted and hurt. And it went on and on undermining her resistance like so much unstable sand, until she was clinging to Jago's shoulders, her own legs unable to support her, her body crying out for the fulfilment his caresses promised.

'Want me?' he whispered against her throat, and she shivered in answering acknowledgement of her need.

His hands slid upwards, cupping her breasts and increasing the dull ache deep inside.

'And you don't love David?'

She stiffened. David! She had completely forgotten him. Forgotten the reason why she had come here in the first place.

'Of course I love him,' she lied desperately. 'And one day you're going to pay for what you did to him!' She tried to pull away, but he wouldn't let her, his mouth ruthlessly plundering hers.

'You're a liar and a coward,' he told her. 'Of course you damn well don't love him. You'd never have responded to me the way you do if you did. But it isn't over, Storm, and when I eventually hold you in my arms and possess your body, it will be my name you cry and not David's.'

His words sent explosions of terror over her body, her mouth faintly swollen as he released her to stare coolly at her heated face.

'I'm late for lunch,' he drawled, shooting back a cuff to glance at his watch.

'And you don't want to keep Miss Townley,' Storm said savagely.

'Jealous?'

'Like hell I am,' Storm said succinctly. 'She's welcome to you. And I don't suppose you'll need to give her any lessons in how to become a woman!'

For a moment his eyes narrowed and she thought she must have betrayed the hurt he had caused her, but he merely said equably, 'I'm sure I won't. Angie has all the right attributes to bring out the male in any man. Even poor David.'

Storm hadn't realised she had clenched her fists until she felt her nails pricking her palms.

'Well, I'm sure you'll be able to entertain one another all afternoon with a mutual exchange of expertise!'

Jago's eyes hardened. 'Don't push me too far, Storm,' he warned. 'For your information I shall be spending most of my time talking business. You should be down on your knees thanking me if you did but know it. Sam was pretty keen for you to join us. He even suggested I might care to spend the afternoon entertaining Angie while he took you on a guided tour of the house he's just bought.'

Storm was powerless to prevent the revulsion from showing in her face.

'Quite,' Jago agreed dryly. 'Sam's no David, and I gained the impression that the afternoon could well end with Mr Townley giving you a prolonged and thorough inspection of his bedroom—and bed.'

He was watching her like a hawk and Storm knew that he was right. Sam was a widower and had been for a good many years. Perhaps another girl might not have quibbled at the thought of an affair with the town's wealthiest citizen, but everything about him repulsed Storm. He made her flesh crawl, and she knew she ought to thank Jago. David had not always been quite as thoughtful and Storm had had to endure several agonising lunches with a view to getting Sam to hold a little less tightly to the purse strings.

'Thank you,' she managed as Jago opened the door for her.

'Did it hurt very much?' he mocked, guessing the effort it had cost her to acknowledge her gratitude.

It had hurt, Storm acknowledged wryly when he had gone, but nowhere near as much as what had happened earlier. What was it about him that got under her skin?

'Lunch?' Pete invited, putting his head round her office door.

Storm shook her head. Pete saw too much and there was no telling what she might reveal to him in her present mood. She wished she had had the forethought to ask David for his friend's phone number. She could have rung him and perhaps the contact might have made their love seem more real.

'I'm going shopping,' she told Pete, trying to banish the disturbing memories of Jago's taunts. 'I want to buy a new dress.'

CHAPTER SIX

PERHAPS it was her preoccupation with her own thoughts, Storm thought wearily as she went from shop to shop, but for some reason there was nothing that really appealed, and after nearly an hour's fruitless examinations of all her favourite boutiques she emerged from the last with nothing to show for her pains apart from aching feet and an empty stomach. A blonde head on the other side of the road caught her eye and her head swivelled automatically, a feeling in the pit of her stomach like a kick from a mule.

What had she been expecting? she asked herself as the girl turned out to be a complete stranger. Jago and Angie? She dismissed the thought, and headed for a small coffee shop she knew in the older part of the town. As she opened the door the smell of freshly roasted coffee beans tormented her taste buds and as she stepped back to allow someone to pass, the window display of a small boutique across the street caught her eye.

Tempted, Storm hovered indecisively on the pavement. She knew the boutique by reputation. It was select and expensive, specialising in the sort of understated clothes that shrieked elegance—and certainly not the place to shop if one was budget-conscious.

There was only one dress in the tiny window, and it made her mouth water. Almost before she knew it she was across the road, opening the door.

The dress, when it was removed from the window, proved to be even more alluring on than it had been off. It was made of chiffon, layers of it, shading from palest grey to smoky violet, a low square neck supported by shoestring straps studded with diamanté, the satin under-

skirt split down one side from thigh to knee. As Storm
moved, the chiffon drifted round her like mist, the colours
as soft and hazy as a winter sky and a perfect foil for her
colouring.

'It's the only one we've got,' the saleswoman told her.
'Mrs Thompson who owns the boutique bought it for herself for an important function, but then she discovered she
was pregnant and by the time the dinner dance comes
round she'll well and truly be bulging!'

Storm laughed. 'Well, her loss is certainly my gain!'
She was steeling herself to ask the price, because she knew
that she had to have the dress. In it she knew that she was
most definitely all woman, and although she told herself
that it was highly unlikely that Jago would ever see her in
it, the merest offchance that he might was enough to make
her reckless enough to buy it. And even then the truth
eluded her.

As it happened the price was quite reasonable, mainly
because the dress was only a size eight and had been
reduced because Mrs Thompson had not thought she
would be able to sell it very easily.

It was half past two when Storm finally got back to the
studio. Sue raised her eyebrows queryingly when she saw
the box, but Storm shook her head.

'No time to chat now,' she mouthed. 'I'm late enough
as it is.'

'Yes, you are, aren't you?' Do you make a habit of
taking one and a half hour lunch breaks?'

Jago! Storm's pulses leapt. She had thought he would
still be at lunch himself, and the intense pleasure that
flooded her at the sound of his voice caught her off guard.

'Sorry,' she apologised huskily, ignoring the surprise in
Sue's eyes. 'I was shopping and . . .'

Was that amusement she saw quirking Jago's mouth?

'Of course,' he agreed dryly, 'I should have known. I
hope it's something sexy. I'm giving a small party shortly,

a sort of housewarming-cum-business affair, and I want everyone from here there. And before you ask me,' he added harshly, 'no, I'm not inviting David.'

Sue was busy with the switchboard and he used the opportunity to remind Storm of the warning he had given her earlier. 'I meant every word I said, Storm,' he told her. 'I mean to have you, and I will.'

Why did she let him affect her? Storm asked herself as she leaned her trembling body against the door of her office. She was a fool for letting him provoke a reaction from her. Her skin was prickling with awareness, and she felt cold and shivery as though she was about to come down with a chill.

Her phone rang and she picked it up, covering the receiver as Jago walked in. He was carrying the advertising figures, and dropped purposefully into a chair as she spoke into the receiver.

'David?' he mouthed sardonically at her.

Her eyes flashed as she glared angrily at him. 'No, my father.'

She expected him to get up and leave, but he merely extended his long legs in front of him, studying her with a thoroughness that discomposed her and made it impossible for her to concentrate on what her father was saying.

He was explaining to her that he would not be able to pick her up until after six.

'I forgot to tell you this morning,' he said, 'I've got a meeting. I've rung your mother and told her we shall be late. What will you do, fill in the time with some shopping?'

'I've got plenty of work to do,' she assured him. 'Don't worry. See you about six, then?'

She hung up and looked at Jago.

'Problems?' he enquired lazily.

Somehow she managed to hold his gaze without betraying how he affected her. In this deceptively mild mood he seemed even more dangerous, his eyes holding all the threat of a momentarily sated tiger's.

'Nothing world-shattering,' she told him coolly. 'My father can't pick me up until six.'

'You could always ring him back and tell him you're going home with me.'

Storm's head jerked up, alarm shimmering in her eyes. 'No, thanks.'

'You used to travel with David,' Jago returned equably. 'I'm going to be living far closer to you than he did. There's no reason why we shouldn't travel together.'

'None at all,' Storm agreed tautly, watching his eyes narrow. 'But we aren't going to.'

'Frightened?' he asked succinctly. 'Of what? That I might carry you off to my lair one dark night? I've told you before . . .' he leaned across the desk, his fingers tilting her chin upwards, 'when I make love to you, Storm, it will be because you want it just as much as I do.'

She forced herself to ignore the warmth spreading through her and the pictures conjured up by his words.

'That will be never,' she told him coldly, watching his mouth harden, his eyes a flinty grey.

'Well, in that case, there's no reason why we shouldn't travel together, is there?'

He had outmanoeuvred her and she knew it. If they travelled together he would use the opportunity to further assault her defences, and there was nothing she could do about it. If she complained he would know that she was aware of him, and if she did not he would just keep re-doubling the attack until she did.

Why? She wasn't beautiful or sexy. He could have his choice of women and he must know it. Was it because she had defied him? Or was it her resolute determination to prefer David to him? She glanced at him from beneath lowered lashes, conscious of the strong moulding of his face. He was constantly deriding David to her, and her breath caught suddenly. Of course, that must be it! He despised David so much it must hurt his pride to know that she preferred him. No doubt he had expected her to fall into his arms long before now. Why not play along with him? Let him think she hadn't guessed why. If he thought he was getting somewhere the pressure might ease off, and she was nearer to cracking under it than she wanted to admit. Let him give her a lift, as long as she played it cool everything would be all right. David would soon be home and when he was they could talk.

'Very well,' she agreed docilely, keeping her eyes veiled.

'You're learning,' Jago told her softly as she dragged her eyes from his mouth, remembering the punishment it could evoke, and hating herself for the spasm of desire that shot through her.

But learning what? she asked herself later, sitting next to her father as they drove home. That it was possible to experience intense desire without the saving grace of love? That a man's body could excite even while his personality repelled? She shuddered and saw her father glance at her.

'Cold?' He turned on the heater. 'Better now?'

Storm smiled gratefully. If only he knew!

They chatted in a desultory fashion, interspersed with comfortable silences. Storm went straight inside while her father put the car away. She found her mother in the kitchen, in a state of intense excitement.

'Thank goodness you're both back! I doubt if I'd have been able to contain myself much longer. You'll never guess what's happened!' she exclaimed, proffering a cheek for her husband to kiss.

'I'm in no mood for guessing games, Mum,' Storm groaned. 'You'll have to tell us.'

'John phoned this afternoon!'

She had their attention now, for telephone calls from

Storm's brother in Australia were something of a rarity.

'There's nothing wrong, is there?' Storm asked anxiously.

Mrs Templeton smiled broadly, 'Far from it. He's getting married—next month! He and Andrea have decided to take the plunge.'

'I didn't even know they were contemplating getting engaged,' said Storm. 'Although I suppose we ought to have guessed. After all, his letters are always full of her.'

'Umm. I did wonder if they might get engaged this Christmas,' Storm's mother agreed. 'But it seems that John has been offered promotion, but the new job is in Perth, so they had to decide between a long courtship or marriage more or less straight away.'

'John married, eh?' Mr Templeton smiled. 'Well, this calls for a celebration. We'll go in the lounge and have a drink and you can tell us exactly what he said,' he told his wife.

Ten minutes later Storm was still trying to come to terms with her mother's news. John married!

'And that's not all.' There was a shade of anxiety in Mrs Templeton's voice, and Storm frowned.

'What else could there be? You're not worried about John marrying Andrea, are you, Mum?'

She was quickly reassured. 'Of course not. She sounds charming. No, the problem is that Andrea's parents have asked your father and me to fly out to Sydney and stay with them until after the wedding. I spoke to Andrea's mother and they seem to have been caught on the hop too. They suspected that an engagement might be in the offing, but they'd no idea that they planned to marry so quickly. However, as this job's come up they realise that Andrea will want to go to Perth with John. They've actually been out there for a weekend already and they both loved the city. John says it's beautiful, and they've managed to find a house.'

4 Exciting Harlequin Presents are yours FREE

SEND NO MONEY MAIL THIS CARD TODAY...

and receive these 4 full-length Harlequin Presents absolutely FREE

Your FREE GIFT Includes

1 SWEET REVENGE by Anne Mather

Antonia innocently became part of a swindle, and Raoul planned to carry out his "sweet revenge." She fled from his castle in Portugal to the security of London... but Raoul, used to having his way, found her.

2 NO QUARTER ASKED by Janet Dailey

All Stacy had been looking for was a place to sort things out for herself. But the beautiful invalid had not reckoned on the ruggedly handsome Cord Harris, powerful Texan cattle baron.

3 GATES OF STEEL by Anne Hampson

Disenchanted with love, Helen fled to Cyprus, only to encounter the handsome Leon Petrou. His proposal surprised Helen, but she accepted. It would be solely a marriage of convenience, she thought. But Helen was wrong.

4 DEVIL IN A SILVER ROOM by Violet Winspear

Paul Cassailis, master of the French château of Satancourt, desired the reserved Margo. But love had brought Margo pain once before. Now Paul stood accused of murder. And Margo discovered to her horror that she loved him.

No one touches the heart of a woman quite like Harlequin.

A HARLEQUIN ROMANCE:

You don't just read it. You live it...

Harlequin Presents romance novels are the ultimate in romantic fiction... the kind of stories you can't put down. They are stories full of the adventures and emotions of love ... full of the hidden turmoil beneath even the most innocent-seeming relationships. Desperate clinging love, emotional conflict, bold lovers, jealousies and romantic imprisonment — you'll find it all in the passionate pages of **Harlequin Presents** romance novels. Let your imagination roam to the far ends of the earth. Meet true-to-life people. Become intimate with those who live larger than life. **Harlequin Presents** romance novels are the kind of books you just can't put down... the kind of experiences that remain in your dreams long after you've read about them.

4 FREE BOOKS FOR YOU

Mail to
Harlequin Reader Service

YES, please send me FREE and without obligation my 4 **Harlequin Presents**. If you do not hear from me after I have examined my 4 FREE books, please send me the 6 new **Harlequin Presents** each month as soon as they come off the presses. I understand that I will be billed only $10.50 for all 6 books. There are no shipping and handling nor any other hidden charges. There is no minimum number of books that I have to purchase. In fact, I can cancel this arrangement at any time. The first 4 books are mine to keep as a FREE gift, even if I do not buy any additional books.

CP164

NAME	(please print)	
ADDRESS		APT. NO.
CITY	STATE/PROV.	ZIP/POSTAL CODE

If under 18, parent or guardian must sign.

This offer is limited to one order per household and not valid to present subscribers. Prices subject to change without notice, offer expires July 31, 1982.

PRINTED IN U.S.A.

**SEND NO MONEY.
MAIL THIS COUPON TODAY
AND RECEIVE
4 FULL-LENGTH
HARLEQUIN PRESENTS
ABSOLUTELY FREE** See other side for details.

'It all sounds idyllic,' Storm broke in, 'so what's the problem?'

'Well, John wants us to fly out as soon as possible, so that he and Andrea can spend some time with us before they get married. And then there's the wedding, and Andrea's mother says we must see something of the country while we're out there, and John wants us to fly up to Perth to see the house. They're spending their honeymoon on the Barrier Reef.' She looked first at her husband and then at Storm. 'I know you'll be able to get time off, Richard, because you were only saying the other day that you could afford to take a few weeks' holiday now that your assistant is settling down so well, but what about you, Storm?'

Storm's heart sank. It was quite out of the question for her to go with her parents. In normal circumstances she might have contemplated asking David for unpaid leave, but if she asked Jago for a month off now he was bound to think she was trying to desert the station. Following in David's footsteps.

'I can't go, Mum,' she said quietly.

Mrs Templeton sighed. 'That's what I thought you'd say,' she admitted. 'If this was just a normal holiday ... but I don't like the thought of leaving you alone here for so long, Storm, and to miss John's wedding.'

Storm's eyes closed. 'I wish I could go, but I can't. You must, though,' she said firmly. 'John would never forgive me if you refused on my account, and he'd have every right. This is a big day for him, and he'll need you there.'

She tried to quell her feeling of disappointment. She would have loved to attend her brother's wedding and meet the girl who was going to be her sister-in-law, but there was just no way that this could be.

Richard Templeton put an arm round his daughter's shoulders. 'Don't worry about it, love,' he told her. 'John will understand. Has he been able to get in touch with Ian?' he asked his wife, across Storm's bowed shoulders.

Mrs Templeton shook her head.

'No. I haven't had a letter from him myself for weeks. The last time he wrote he said he was just about to fly out to Africa to investigate the possibility of some new oilfields out there. I suppose he must still be there.'

The Templeton's were used to long silences from their second son when he was out in the field and had learned not to be worried by them.

'Well, he must have quite a lot of leave due to him,' Richard Templeton commented. 'It's a pity we can't get in touch with him. It looks as though our side of the family is going to be very scantily represented at the wedding!'

Naturally John's marriage was the sole topic of conversation during the evening. Mrs Templeton was torn between excitement and dismay.

'We shall miss your birthday,' she said to Storm at one point. 'And Christmas, unless we fly home right after the wedding.'

'You'll do no such thing,' Storm told her firmly. 'Although I shall expect an extra special present, for my forbearance!'

It was a pity that John's promotion meant the wedding had to be arranged so hurriedly, she decided as she prepared for bed, but she wasn't going to have her mother spoil the occasion for herself by worrying about her. She was twenty-two, after all, and more than capable of looking after herself for four weeks. Against her will her eyes were drawn to Jago's house. A light shone in one of the upstairs rooms and she felt the heat rise on her skin as she thought of him in bed.

This was crazy, she told herself, feeling the increased thud of her heart and the ache that spread slowly upwards. Physical desire, that's all it was, she told herself fiercely. She loved *David*, for God's sake. Safe, protective David!

But when she fell asleep it was of Jago that she dreamed, small heated moans falling from her lips as she thrashed feverishly from side to side.

'Are you sure you won't mind being left on your own, Storm?' her mother asked anxiously in the morning.

In the middle of her coffee Storm shook her head. She heard the powerful purr of Jago's car outside and grabbed for her coat, putting her cup down.

'Perhaps your father could have a word with Mr Marsh,' she persisted. 'If he explained Mr Marsh might . . .'

'No, Mum,' Storm said firmly. 'Now stop worrying.'

'I suppose it's only natural that we should worry more about you than we did about the boys,' Richard Templeton said from behind his paper. 'Old-fashioned of us, I expect, in this day and age, but then parents are. This house can be very lonely in the winter. Your nearest neighbour is nearly half a mile away, after all.'

Storm's heart started thumping erratically. Her nearest neighbour was Jago, and for some reason she found that she did not want him to know that she was going to be alone in the house. Fear that he might redouble his assault upon her defences?

'Jago's here,' she said unnecessarily to her parents as his dark head passed the window. 'I'd better go. At least travelling with the boss means that no one can bawl you out for being late!'

'And gives me time to finish my breakfast,' her father added. 'Heard anything from David, by the way?'

'He's due back at the end of the week,' Storm said, avoiding the question. 'I expect I'll see him then.'

The inside of Jago's car smelled disturbingly masculine, and although she tried to relax she was unbearably aware of the man sitting next to her.

'Heard from David?' he asked smoothly, unconsciously repeating her father's question.

'No. Not that it's any business of yours,' Storm told him.

His eyes left the road to rest coolly on her heated face. 'Maybe there's more to him than I thought,' he drawled sardonically. 'You're showing all the signs of frustration this morning. Or isn't David the cause?'

'Don't speak to me like that!' Storm demanded, hating the way he seemed to get under her skin. 'If you must know I'm feeling a little out of sorts because my brother's getting married and I shan't be able to attend the wedding.' Now why had she told him that? She bit her lip and stared out of the car window.

'Oh?'

His voice invited her to tell him more, but she refused, turning the conversation instead to the progress she was making with the Harmer advertisement.

'I've got a dummy tape ready. Pete's taking it over this morning.'

'Pete? Can't you go yourself?'

'I could, but I've got an appointment at the local children's home. We're trying to set up a programme featuring some of the children—something for Christmas. Unless, of course, you have any objections.'

'You might freeze David with that cool little voice, my dear,' Jago told her lightly, 'but it has no effect at all upon me. I'm surprised you aren't following up the lead young Harmer gave you, though. He was definitely interested.' He shot her a sideways look, but Storm stared rigidly ahead.

'Well, I'm not,' she told him. 'Neither in him, nor you, nor anyone else, except David.'

She expected him to be annoyed, but was not prepared for the inimical rage leaping to life in his eyes.

'Oh yes, you are,' he told her suavely, 'and I could

damn well prove it to you here and now, if I wanted to.
Or is that what you're hoping for? Tough luck, Storm,'
he drawled. 'The next time you're going to be making all
the moves and doing all the asking.'

'Never!' Storm gritted at him as he slid the car into the
car-park. 'Never, never, never!'

His laughter floated after her and she hurried into the
building, her body on fire as though with a fever, but her
hands as cold as ice. He was deliberately trying to break
her, she thought bitterly. Well, he wouldn't succeed!

The children's home was on the edge of the town, but
as it was a pleasant day, with the sun shining pale lemon
in a soft blue sky and the leaves lying crisp and autumnal
on the ground, Storm elected to walk there instead of
getting a taxi.

The house had been left to the council by an eccentric
local landlord, whose own sons had been killed during the
First World War. Large and rambling, the huge Victorian
mansion took a large slice of the council's rate income in
upkeep, but the money was well spent, Storm thought
appreciatively as she gave her name at the gatehouse and
waited to be admitted.

With the house were several acres of land and also a
small home farm which provided eggs and vegetables for
the home as well as giving the children a grounding in
animal care and gardening.

Even so, despite the generous bequest of its original
owner and the undoubted care of the local authority, the
house had an unmistakably 'institutional' air, Storm
thought as she was shown into a small waiting room. In
the distance she could hear the muted hum of children's
voices. Chipped paintwork and shabby furniture bore mute
testimony to the fact that money was obviously desperately needed, and Storm wondered what it must be like
to be brought up in a place like this, without the love of a
mother or father—in fact, with no one to call one's own.

Of course the staff would do their best—this was no Dickensian 'workhouse', and yet weren't the children who inhabited this house as deprived as Dicken's Oliver Twist had been, albeit in a different fashion? Storm wondered. It was a sobering thought. She was conscience-stricken to realise how little thought she had ever given to the plight of these children. Of course they were well fed, well clothed and properly educated, but what about their emotional needs? What about every child's occasional need to come first?

These were questions she put to the Matron, when, eventually she was shown into her office.

'You've hit the nail well and truly on the head,' she was told. 'An orphanage, no matter how well run, or how excellently staffed, can never hope to take the place of a real home. This is why we're always so keen to find foster-homes for our children. With the babies of course there's never any problem, but it's the others—the older children, the ones with difficult backgrounds; these are the ones my heart aches for.'

Storm listened sympathetically. Mary Simmonds reminded her of one of her own junior schoolteachers, scrupulously fair, a disciplinarian who nevertheless recognised the children's need for love and affection.

'So really, what you're saying is that for the general public to simply send a teddy-bear at Christmas and fill a sack with their own kids' cast-offs is not really what's needed?'

An idea was beginning to take root, but before she could voice it Storm wanted to be sure she had not misunderstood. In answer to her question Mary Simmonds said quickly,

'Don't get me wrong, we're grateful for everything that people do already, but our real need is for the children to experience true family life, even if it's only the odd weekend here and there.' She broke off to scan Storm's thoughtful face. 'Why do you ask?'

'I was just thinking that instead of encouraging people to donate to the home we could perhaps encourage them to sponsor individual children as adopted "aunties and uncles". I realise it won't be easy. Anyone who was interested would have to be thoroughly checked out, and then there's the problem of ensuring that they won't lose interest and leave the child feeling even more deprived than ever, but I think it could work . . .'

'So do I,' Mary Simmonds pronounced delightedly. 'It's a wonderful idea, Storm. Mr Marsh told me that I would find you very helpful, but this——! What will you do? Launch a public appeal?'

'I was thinking of something along those lines,' Storm admitted, 'although I shall have to check with Mr Marsh first, to get his approval.'

'I should think you'll find him extremely sympathetic and helpful,' Mary Simmonds surprised her by saying. 'When I spoke to him he was most emphatic that the station wanted to do all it could to help us. I suppose it's a reflection on his own childhood, and from what he told me the children's home where he was brought up was nothing like as pleasant as this one.'

Storm stared at her. She knew that Jago had been in touch with the orphanage concerning the programmes they were planning to do, but she had had no idea that he himself had been brought up in a children's home. His air of moneyed ease was so much a part of him that she had somehow taken it for granted that he had been born with the proverbial silver spoon clenched firmly between his teeth. She was a fool, she told herself scornfully, suppressing a momentary pang. Jago Marsh had no need of her sympathy and would probably ridicule her were she ever stupid enough to proffer it.

Mary Simmonds gave her a worried glance. 'You didn't know about Mr Marsh, did you? I wish I hadn't said anything, but . . .'

'Don't worry about it,' Storm told her. 'I shan't repeat it to anyone.'

Plainly relieved, the Matron allowed herself to be side-tracked into questions about the children's routine, while Storm made notes which she hoped would be useful when she came to organise how best to launch their appeal. Finding suitable foster families for the children promised to be a time-consuming task, but there was no doubt in her mind that the end result—even if that was only one child provided with a 'family'—would more than outweigh the hard work. Storm only had to think of her own comparatively privileged childhood to harden her determination to do all she could for these less fortunate children.

By the time she was ready to leave, they had drafted out an outline which Storm intended to put before Jago. If he agreed, the disc jockeys could spend a few minutes at the beginning of each session talking about the home and its needs, without making any attempt to glamorise the foster-families' role in the lives of the children. Mentally making a note to ask Jago about taking photographs of some of the children to pin up in their foyer and to check with the local social services departments to get their reaction, Storm collected her notebook and bag.

'You can't know what it would mean to all of us here if we could provide the older children especially with some form of family support. They have to leave here when they're sixteen, often without any proper training for a job or anywhere to stay. It's hard enough for any youngster these days, never mind these children!'

Storm agreed with her, and yet as she walked back to the studio, scuffing her feet in the dry leaves, she couldn't help reflecting that Jago had somehow managed to overcome all the obstacles and achieve the patina of success. But what lay beneath that patina? As a child he had known rejection and as an adult adulation, but had he ever experienced the range of emotions that lay in between?

The thought held her, returning at odd moments when her mind should have been on other things. Jago was a determined adversary, that she already knew, and she would be a fool to let sympathy for the child he had once been come between her and her desire to keep him at arms' length.

CHAPTER SEVEN

STORM's parents were flying to Sydney at the weekend, and she was pleased when David rang her on Thursday to suggest that they go out for a meal on Saturday evening. The build-up to her parents' departure would leave her with a sense of anticlimax once they had gone, and although she had plenty of work to occupy her mind she felt that she would prefer to be out of the house.

On Friday morning Jago arrived while she was finishing her breakfast, and Mrs Templeton invited him inside and offered him a cup of coffee.

'Sorry I'm late,' Storm apologised, gulping hers down, surprised when he gave her a lazy smile and told her there was no rush.

'Actually I think I'm early,' he told her. 'I've got to go to London this morning, so I thought I'd get an early start.'

London? Storm's heart thudded against her ribs. Had he changed his mind and perhaps decided that he had had enough of Radio Wyechester and its problems?

'Looks like someone else is off somewhere,' he added, eyeing the luggage stacked up in the hall.

'My parents are off to Australia. My brother is getting married,' Storm told him curtly, as he accepted the cup of coffee her mother had poured for him. She could smell the clean sharp scent of his after-shave, and the dark hair was faintly damp as though he had recently showered. The thought made her stomach lurch betrayingly, the hand holding her coffee cup shaking at the disturbing images projected by her mind. She had never fantasised about the male body before in her life, and that it should be Jago Marsh who should cause her to do so made her tremble with nervous fear. He had turned her neatly ordered world upside down, but she was damned if she would let him find out.

'Yes. We're leaving tomorrow,' Mrs Templeton chipped in excitedly. 'I'm looking forward to the wedding, of course, but I do worry about leaving Storm here alone. This house is so remote, and we'll be gone at least six weeks.'

'Mother!' Storm protested warningly, not daring to look at Jago's face, but it was already too late.

'Don't worry about it any more,' Jago assured Mrs Templeton. 'I'll make sure I check the house every night when I drop Storm off. I'm only ten minutes away if she needs me.'

He looked at Storm, and her legs went terribly weak, a feeling like nothing she had known before sweeping over her.

'I'm sure I shan't,' she told him coolly. 'After all, David is coming back today and . . .'

'Storm!' her mother reproached, turning back to Jago. 'Don't listen to her, Mr Marsh,' she smiled. 'It would put my mind at rest if you would keep an eye on her. David is a dear, but he does live five miles away. I'll feel much happier knowing that she isn't completely alone.'

As she followed Jago out to the car five minutes later Storm was seething with resentment at the way her mother had manipulated the conversation, but under the resentment lurked fear, and she knew it was this that made her move restlessly in her seat, trying not to look at the determined thrust of Jago's shoulders beneath the immaculate dark suit.

'I could have made my own way to Wyechester if you'd told me you wanted to go to London,' she said to him as he negotiated the drive.

He stopped at the bottom, casting her a brief, amused glance, then frowned suddenly as he switched off the engine and leaned across to her.

She shrank back, her eyes widening nervously, fear trembling through her as she felt his fingers brush her blouse.

Her eyes closed automatically. There was a faint click and when she opened them again Jago was starting the car.

'You forgot your seat belt,' he said urbanely, and as the hot colour flooded her cheeks, Storm cursed herself for her betraying reaction. He must have known she thought he was going to kiss her! She bit her lower lip, willing the colour to fade from her face.

'You must be disappointed at missing your brother's wedding,' Jago remarked when they had joined the main stream of traffic.

Storm would have preferred to remain silent; the intimacy of the car was oppressive and she wondered if Jago was as aware of her as she was of him. Hardly, she thought bitterly. To him it was all a game that he was intent on winning and making her subtly aware of him at every turn was just another tactic.

'Yes, I am,' she admitted, forcing a cool smile. 'But of course I couldn't ask for the time off.'

'Couldn't, or wouldn't?' Jago asked softly. 'You wouldn't like to be in debt to me, would you, Storm? If dear David had still been Controller, I'm sure you'd have asked him. So he's back, is he? Seeing him tonight, are you?'

'No,' Storm said shortly, ruffled despite her struggle to remain cool and unaffected by his taunts.

'No? Have dinner with me, then,' Jago said silkily.

Thrown completely off guard, Storm stared at him. 'But you'll be in London.'

'Only for a few hours.'

'I can't come with you,' she told him firmly. 'Tonight is my parents' last evening at home. They'll want me to stay with them.'

'Convenient. What about Saturday, then?'

Storm took a deep breath. He was deliberately trying

to needle her, she thought. 'On Saturday I'm having dinner with David.'

'Somewhere romantic and secluded,' Jago mocked, 'and then home to an empty house where you can be alone . . .'

'David isn't like you,' Storm said unwisely. 'He has other things on his mind besides sex . . .'

'More fool him,' Jago said crudely. 'And more fool you. Have you really never questioned his lack of desire for you, or yours for him?'

They were turning into the car-park and Storm refused to answer, wrenching the door open the moment Jago stopped and hurrying away from him.

He caught up with her just as she reached the building, his fingers tightening on her wrist like an iron band. She looked upwards and saw anger, intermingled with another emotion that made her mouth go dry with dread.

Jago wanted her, and he was going to use every means at his disposal to remind her of that fact, until she convinced him that he was wasting his time—or she gave in. Her knees threatened to buckle under her, and she pulled away from him. Instinct warned her that to fight him now would only increase his determination. A feeling of panic began to rise inside her. David did desire her and she him; it just wasn't the be-all and end-all of their relationship. David was not the type to force himself on anyone, he would need encouragement and a definite go-ahead before he put their relationship on a more intimate footing.

She had forgotten that Jago was still watching her, and cried out as his grasp tightened, the colour leaving her face as his hands clamped on to her shoulders, shaking her as though she were a rag doll.

'I know exactly what's going through your mind,' Jago told her grimly, his lips white with anger, 'Just don't forget that your mother has appointed me as your guardian, Storm, a duty I intend to take extremely seriously, so forget any thoughts of taking dear David home with you. It wouldn't work anyway,' he told her cruelly. 'Like I've already said, he doesn't want you, and I doubt if you'd find him much of a lover even if he did.'

'Not like you, of course!' snapped Storm, thrusting him away, her whole body shaking with the force of the emotion erupting inside her. Emotion conjured up by his words, and their effect on her senses, which like it or not she was powerless to deny.

'I know what you're trying to do,' she told him shakily as she turned away. 'But it won't work.'

She hurried into the office before he could say anything else, responding automatically to Sue's smile.

Her morning was busy; the phone seldom stopped ringing, and she had promised to spend half an hour in one of the studios with Pete going over the approach they were going to take with the foster-parent scheme. Jago had already given it his approval, and Pete was keen to make as much use of the time left to them before Christmas as possible.

When he and Storm had finished discussing the details Storm stretched and glanced at her watch.

'Nearly lunch-time. Where does the day go? Did Jago say anything to you about why he was going to London?'

She hadn't intended to ask him. In fact she had been determined not to betray any interest at all. If he was going to leave them in the lurch and return to his own business interests, well, so much the better; that was what she had told herself, but she held her breath while she waited for Pete's reply.

'I didn't know he was going,' he said. 'Perhaps it's something to do with the new finance he's promised us. Things are certainly moving now.'

Storm bit her lip, unable to deny it. Jago's dynamic approach achieved far better results than David's milder one had done.

'Are you sure he's gone to London?' Pete added. 'Sue was in here half an hour ago and she said something about him being in rather a bad mood. I know he did go out, but I got the impression it would only be for an hour or so.'

Storm shrugged. What did it matter where he was? She had intended to make do with a sandwich at her desk for lunch, but the small enclosed room was stuffy and on impulse she took her sandwiches to the local park, enjoying the late autumn sunshine.

When she got back Sue pounced on her, round-eyed and ruffled. 'Where have you been? Mr Marsh has been looking everywhere for you. He's furious!'

In spite of herself Storm felt her stomach lurch.

'Really?' she said coolly to Sue, trying to pretend she wasn't worried. 'I am entitled to my lunch.'

'He said to tell you to go straight to his office the moment you got back,' Sue added.

What on earth had she done? Storm thought, discarding her coat and checking her hair. Every step of the new campaigns they were planning had been submitted to Jago for his approval and she could think of nothing she had done to merit being sent for in this arbitrary fashion. The thought cheered her, helping her to smile calmly as she knocked and walked into Jago's office five minutes later.

He was seated at his desk, bent over some papers. Without looking at her he said coldly, 'I thought I said you were to come straight here.'

'I had to take my coat off,' Storm replied, willing herself to appear calm. The sight of his dark hair reminded her of the feel of it beneath her fingers. Banishing the memory, she waited for him to speak. He kept on reading, the tense atmosphere in the small room becoming more tangible by the minute.

On the desk Storm could see a letter from Harmers, and tried idly to read it upside down. No doubt it was Mr

Harmer's agreement to their advertising terms. She had been working hard on his campaign and hoped to have it ready to show to him before the end of the month.

'I've nearly finished the Harmer campaign,' she said chattily when Jago folded his papers. Although she was loathe to admit it, the silence he was maintaining was making her feel acutely nervous. Another of his ploys? she wondered a little acidly. It was certainly having its effect; she felt as nervous as a junior summoned before the Chairman of the Board.

'You didn't go to London, then?' she ventured when he continued to say nothing.

The file of papers was thrown into a drawer which he closed with a decisive slam, his eyes as cold and merciless as a winter sky as he motioned to the chair in front of him.

'No, I didn't. I suppose you thought you had it all neatly planned, didn't you? But fortunately young Harmer had the sense to phone me and tell me what was going on. For your information I've wasted an entire morning trying to retrieve the situation you and Winters so carefully set up. My God!' he said suddenly, 'I know how you feel about me—you've made that perfectly obvious, but I never thought you'd go to the lengths of sabotaging the station just to get one up on me!'

'Sabotaging?' Storm stared at him. 'I don't know what you're talking about, Jago,' she told him blankly. 'What am I supposed to have done?'

'Don't act the innocent with me!' he snapped harshly, getting up and pacing the narrow strip of floor between his desk and the window. With his back to her Storm was at liberty to let her eyes dwell hungrily on the muscular breadth of his shoulders tapering to the lean waist and powerful legs.

'You deliberately fed Winters information about the campaign we were planning for Harmers so that he could ruin it. Harmer told me himself, so don't try denying it,' he added acidly. 'Was that what the pair of you planned to celebrate on Saturday? Well, it hasn't worked. I've managed to convince Mr Harmer that not only can we produce the campaign on time but also that it will be properly run. I also assured him that he need have no fear that we were in any danger of going bankrupt without our major backer. I've already arranged fresh finance . . . What did you have to give Sam Townley to get him to withdraw his support, or can I guess?' he sneered. 'No wonder you didn't baulk at the thought of David as a lover when . . .'

'Stop it! Stop it!' Storm was trembling with rage. She got up and stood in front of him, her eyes smoky purple as she stared up into his face.

'I haven't the faintest idea what you're talking about. I didn't know Sam Townley was withdrawing his support. I did tell David about the Harmer campaign, but only because I knew he was interested in how we were doing. It was no secret; but to suggest that either he or I would deliberately try to dissuade Mr Harmer from giving us the go-ahead . . .' Her voice mirrored her disbelief.

Cold grey eyes searched her face.

'You must believe me, Jago. I love my job here, and besides,' she added proudly, 'if I did want to get at you, as you put it, I wouldn't do it in such an underhand manner.'

He watched her broodingly for several minutes, then turned back to the window.

'I admit that it isn't quite your style,' he agreed at last. 'But nothing you can say will convince me of Winters' innocence. Harmer himself told me that Winters went to see him. To talk about the campaign, he told him, but what it turned out to be was a warning that Radio Wyechester was about to come to a sticky end and that he'd be a fool to tie himself to any advertising agreement with us.'

'No!' Storm cried disbelievingly. 'You're just saying

that because you despise David. He would never do anything like that. You don't know him like I do . . .'

'No, Storm,' Jago said heavily, turning to face her, 'you
don't know him. Go to him. Ask him, although I suppose
he'll lie to you, and you like a fool will believe him. Well,
you can tell him from me that it won't work. Sam Townley's loss is no big deal, and Harmer has agreed to give
us a chance. When I told him the circumstances under
which David left the station, he was more than ready to
agree that it was probably a question of sour grapes.'

Storm's face burned. 'You maligned David to him like
that?'

'I told him the truth,' Jago interrupted harshly. 'You
stubborn little fool, can't you see? Your David wanted to
ruin this station; if I were a vindictive man I could
probably drag him through the courts for what he's tried
to do, but I'm not. As it is I should have been in London
today at an important meeting . . .'

Storm was close to tears. She clenched her fists, staring
resentfully at his inflexible back.

'I wish you had been,' she said bitterly, 'and I wish you
would go there now and never come back. And as for
your accusations,' she fought against the tears thickening
her voice and said huskily, 'I won't ask you to take them
back, because I don't care what you think of me. I'll go
and write out my notice and . . .'

She didn't get any further. Jago swung round, gripping
her arms, his eyes almost black as they swept her face.

'Oh no, you don't! You've got a twelve-month contract
with the station with over ten months to go, and don't
you forget it. I want you here, Storm, where I can keep
an eye on you. Now get out of here before I do something
we'll both regret,' he told her curtly.

How she got to her office Storm did not know. She sat
down, feeling sick and shaken. How could he have thought
that she would deliberately . . .? Tears filled her eyes and

she let them fall. She dialled David's number and got no response. He was probably in Oxford. If tonight hadn't been her parents' last evening at home she would have driven round to see him. Her parents! She mustn't let them see how upset she was, otherwise her mother would be worrying the whole time she was away. If only she hadn't signed that contract two months ago, but it was binding and she knew she could not get out of it. She couldn't understand why Jago wanted to keep her, thinking what he did, she thought bitterly. She would have thought he would be glad to get rid of her.

On a sudden impulse she dialled Harmers' number and asked to speak to Greg. He sounded pleased to hear from her, and rather uncertainly she explained why she was phoning.

'David Winters did come to see us,' he admitted when she asked him outright. 'My father was a bit alarmed when he told us that both he and Sam Townley were pulling out of the radio station because of lack of faith in Jago Marsh. Actually my father had been quite impressed with him and with your campaign, but when David told him how Jago was planning to cut corners . . .'

Storm closed her eyes, disbelievingly, the receiver sticky and damp in her hand.

'You still there?' Greg asked anxiously.

Her throat dry, she croaked an assent.

'Of course it's all sorted out now,' Greg assured her. 'Jago came over to see my father this morning. Once he knew that Jago was investing in the station himself and that contrary to what Winters said there would be more money for development and not less, it restored his faith. I must admit what Winters told us gave us quite a jolt, but we'd no reason to disbelieve him . . . Actually I nearly rang you at the time, but I didn't want to involve you, and Winters told us that you weren't at all happy with the way things were being run.'

They chatted for a few minutes and eventually Storm
hung up, staring sightlessly at the wall. How could David
have done it? And to use her! But there must be some
explanation, some reason. She shuddered suddenly, picking up some papers and opening the door.

She owed Jago an apology, which she must give him
before she lost her courage, but nothing he could say
would make her believe that David had acted through
malice or a deliberate intention of ruining the station.

She knocked on his door, and opened it. He was staring
out of the window, as he had been when she left, but he
had removed his jacket which was draped over his chair.
She could see the ripple of his muscles beneath the thin
silk shirt, and her heart started pounding so loudly she
felt sure he must hear it.

'Yes?'

He looked through her rather than at her, and Storm
wetted her dry lips with the tip of her tongue.

'If you've come to ask me to release you from your
contract, forget it,' he told her roughly. 'What I said
before stands.'

'No, it isn't that.' Even to her own ears her voice
sounded nervously husky, and she saw his eyes narrow as
they took in her clenched hands and pale face. 'I've come
to apologise,' she said before her courage deserted her.
'I've spoken to Greg Harmer and he told me . . .'

He was still looking at her with that same steely impersonal stare, and she took a deep breath, wishing she
could match his self-control.

'He told me much the same as you did,' she said quietly.
'I can see why you thought that David and I . . .' Her
voice shook and she had to take another deep breath. 'I
can see why you were so ready to blame us, but there
must be some explanation. David would never . . .'

'Damn you!' Jago snarled suddenly. 'Even now you leap
to his defence. "There must be some explanation,"' he

mimicked savagely. 'There's an explanation all right, but you're too stubborn to accept it. Winters wanted to make things as difficult for me as possible and has done right from the start. When the I.B.A. asked me to step in and try and salvage something from the wreckage he'd made of this place, I didn't want to, and I told them so. But they have ways of bringing pressure to bear and . . .'

'The I.B.A. asked you? But David told me he confided in you, quite by chance, and that you . . .'

'I was called in by the I.B.A. when the results of the random rating tests they'd done in this area, prior to reviewing your licence, came through. Only the fact that I knew David from the B.B.C. made me agree to help him out. I even offered to invest in the station, but he told me he already had enough backing.'

'But . . . but . . .'

'But you didn't have anywhere near enough. Oh yes, I discovered that for myself the moment I arrived here,' Jago agreed grimly. 'Whereupon Winters promptly resigned, probably hoping I'd back off and the I.B.A. would be forced to reinstate him. For God's sake, can't you *see* what manner of man he is? Or don't you care? Doesn't it bother you that he's weak, a liar . . .' He broke off to stare at her in mingled anger and exasperation. 'Why do I bother? You don't want a real man, do you, Storm, you're more than happy to let David shelter behind you . . . using you . . .'

Storm tried to ignore what he was saying and his criticisms of David—criticism she kept telling herself could surely not be valid.

'What about Sam Townley?' she asked him.

'Another of David's little tricks. Your David's been a busy man while he's been in Oxford. He and Townley were in this together. No doubt they expected to pick up the franchise for the station quite easily once they'd disposed of me. Townley probably discovered that I couldn't raise enough finance to carry the full burden of this station, but what he forgot to take into account is that I have friends who can.'

'So you're now financially in control of the station as well?'

Jago grimaced at her bitter tone. 'It's quite normal and above board. David had money in the venture, and I'm a long way from being the only shareholder, but yes, since you ask, now I am in control.'

'I'm surprised you want to keep me to my contract in view of my relationship with David,' Storm said sarcastically. 'Only an hour ago you were ready to accuse me of trying to ruin the station, and yet . . .'

'It was a logical deduction,' he told her dryly. 'After all, you've never stopped ramming David down my throat. But whatever your other failings you are good at your job. Your campaigns have flair and originality, but don't expect David to be pleased when he finds out I'm holding you to your contract.'

'I'm sure he won't be,' Storm returned coolly. 'His girl-friend working for the man who ruined him. I can't say I blame him either.'

Jago smiled, his eyes cold. 'You are a fool, aren't you?' he said softly. 'David doesn't give a damn about you, Storm. Angie Townley's more his idea of something warm and cuddly to take to bed. No, he was just using you to get at me. He knew damn well I'd think you were implicated in his nasty little schemes and he knows you well enough to gauge your reaction when I faced you with it. I'll bet right at this moment he's congratulating himself on having lost the station its advertising department. The I.B.A. has granted me a temporary licence for twelve months and I wouldn't be at all surprised if, at the end of that time, David and Townley hoped to have a nice little package put together to get the franchise back again.'

'You're wrong. I know you're wrong,' Storm told him.

Faint fingers of sunshine touched the strong column of his throat and she couldn't help comparing the tanned firmness of his skin with David's pallid, unhealthy flesh. She pushed the thought away, appalled by the instinctive leaping of her senses and the overwhelming desire to go up to him and place her lips against that bared flesh. For a moment she almost fainted with the shock of what was happening to her. It was desire, she told herself helplessly; physical desire, that was all; and the demanding urgency of it confirmed all her worst fears about herself.

In some secret part of her she had always known she could feel like this, and she had always feared the power of an emotion that would hold her in chains against her will, making her a slave to its rapacious demands.

'Storm?' Jago was watching her with a glint in his eyes that made her wonder how much she had betrayed. 'Go home early,' he told her abruptly. 'I'll take you myself. I have some business to catch up with, but I can work as well at home as I can here. Get your coat.'

She wanted to refuse, but somehow the words would not come. She felt as though she were living in a dream—a dream, more like a nightmare! In her office she dialled David's number again, listening to the repetitive ring and hanging up with a faint sigh. Obviously he wasn't there.

He couldn't have done those dreadful things. He couldn't be planning to ruin the station. Surely he would have given her some hint . . . some warning . . .

Jago drove her home in silence, and as Storm stepped out of the car she mentally braced her shoulders, telling herself that she must not cast any shadows on her parents' last evening at home.

As she had suspected Mrs Templeton had gone to a good deal of trouble over dinner.

'You're early!' she exclaimed when Storm walked into the kitchen. 'Has Mr Marsh gone?' When Storm said that he had she sighed. 'I was going to ask him to have dinner with us. A little thank you for offering to keep an eye on you while we're away. Men who live on their own appreciate the odd family meal.'

Storm laughed. 'Oh, Mum, Jago Marsh doesn't need mothering,' she told her. 'I'll bet he's got women lining up to cook his meals.'

'I don't know what you've got against him. I thought he was charming.'

Her parents were flying from Heathrow, and Storm went with them to wave them off. Driving her father's car back along the empty country roads during the afternoon, she made a detour to the village where David lived. All at once she couldn't wait until the evening to find out what had been going on.

His car was parked outside and she gave a sigh of relief. At least he was in.

She knocked on the door and in due course he appeared, dressed in faded baggy jeans and an old sweater.

'Storm!' He looked surprised and, Storm thought, biting her lip, not very pleased.

'Is something wrong?' he asked, stepping to one side so that she could enter the small living room. The table was covered in papers and Storm glanced at them, noticing David's flurried tidying up.

'I've been trying to ring you since yesterday,' she began, looking round for an empty chair.

'I've been busy. Couldn't whatever it is wait until tonight?'

'Busy? With work on the shop in Oxford?'

There was a momentary hesitation, then he said evasively, 'Yes. Well, now that you're here I'll make a cup of tea.'

No welcome kiss, Storm noticed ruefully, no attempt to take her in his arms, even though it was several days since she had seen him. On an impulse she stood up, going up to him and sliding her arms round his neck.

'Don't I get a kiss?' she asked softly. David's cottage fronted on to the main road; and as he bent his head rather awkwardly she caught a familiar dark green flash as a car drove by, and Jago's eyes met hers for a brief second before he disappeared.

She tried to find the familiar comfort in David's embrace, but it wasn't there, probably never had been there except in her imagination, and she guessed from the hurried manner in which he released her that he was aware of it too.

'David, I came here this afternoon because I wanted to talk to you,' she said quietly. 'Jago told me yesterday that you'd tried to prevent us from getting the Harmer contract.'

'And you believed him, of course,' David said bitterly. 'Has he managed to get you into his bed yet?' The crudity of his words held Storm silent with shock, and her face drained of colour.

'No, of course he hasn't,' she told him angrily. 'Surely you don't think I would do something like that?'

'He's made it pretty clear what he wants from you,' David told her sulkily, 'and what he wants he usually gets.'

David was jealous of Jago, Storm admitted uneasily, but the jealousy had nothing to do with her. It went far deeper than that, and a fear that could not be reasoned away rose up inside her.

'David, you didn't do all those things, did you?' she asked shakily. 'You didn't tell Mr Harmer that we were going bankrupt, or. . . .'

'What does it matter if I did?' David asked bitterly. 'It's no more than Marsh deserves. The station was mine until he came along. The I.B.A. had no right to put him in over my head, and—yes, all right,' he said fiercely, 'I wanted to make things difficult for him, to give him a taste of the problems I'd had to face. When you told me about the Harmer campaign it seemed the ideal starting point . . .'

She must not be sick, Storm thought, oppressed by the atmosphere of the small room and the man seated opposite her, who had suddenly become a stranger.

'And the bookshop?' she asked him faintly.

He had the grace to look faintly ashamed. 'There isn't one, but I had to have some reason for leaving.'

'So that you and Sam Townley could make a bid to take over the franchise when it comes up next year?'

'Why the hell shouldn't we?' David asked defiantly, shattering Storm's frail hope that there could still be some reasonable explanation of what had happened.

'Oh, David!' she exclaimed unhappily. 'Sam Townley, of all people . . .'

'There's nothing wrong with Sam,' David said defensively. 'Angie's sure she can persuade him . . .'

'Angie?' Storm stared at him. Had Jago been doing more than just baiting her when he said that David would prefer to take Angie to bed than her? One look at his face told her all she needed to know. Pain twisted inside her like a knife.

'So even that wasn't real,' she said bitterly. 'You never actually wanted me, did you, David? You didn't love me as I thought . . .'

'I'm sorry,' he said awkwardly. 'I'm fond of you, Storm, and always have been, but you can't pretend we ever set the world alight.' His mouth twisted wryly. 'I'll admit when we first met I used to wonder what you'd be like in bed, but when I got to know you I realised it just wasn't on.'

'And does Angie set the world alight for you?' Storm asked savagely, biting her lip when she saw the colour filling his thin face. 'I'm sorry,' she apologised, 'I shouldn't have said that. I must go . . .'

'You do understand, don't you, Storm?' he pleaded with

her at the door. 'I had no choice, I had to make Marsh see that he couldn't walk all over me, and as for the rest—well, it's not my fault if I can't get excited about you. You never gave me any encouragement, and . . .'

'It isn't your fault, David,' Storm said quietly as she stepped outside.

She was grateful for the fact that she had parked the car down a side street from David's house, because that gave her the opportunity to sit quietly in it until the shaking had gone.

She couldn't cry, it hurt too much for that. Even now she could hardly believe it. And the thing that hurt most, she acknowledged, was not that David didn't love her—deep inside she had known that all along—but that he liked her so little that he could willingly have used her as a dupe. And a dupe was what she had been, there could be no mistake about that.

She didn't go straight home. The empty house was something she felt unable to face in her present mood, and instead she drove for a while, letting her thoughts drift and her mind exhaust itself as she tried to rationalise what she had learned.

David had not deliberately tried to hurt her, she told herself, but the way he had talked about her had stripped away her defences.

He might not actually have accused her of being cold and unfeminine, she thought wryly, but he had left her in no doubt that that was what he considered she was. And yet she had responded readily enough to Jago. Too readily, she thought sombrely as she drove home.

CHAPTER EIGHT

THE evening stretched emptily ahead of her. She had intended to wash her hair and have a leisurely bath before David picked her up, but now there seemed little point in going to all that trouble just to sit in front of the fire and watch television.

She found a book that her mother had been reading, but it failed to hold her attention and after a while she went upstairs to wash her hair, thinking that the occupation would keep her hands busy if not her mind.

Even now she was finding it hard to take it in. She had just finished rinsing her hair when she heard the doorbell, and thinking it must be David come to explain that it was all a misunderstanding she flew downstairs and opened the door.

Jago stood on the doorstep, immaculately dressed in dress shirt and dinner suit.

'So you are in.' He was frowning and Storm was self-consciously aware of her wet hair and old jeans.

'I'm just getting ready to go out,' she lied, watching the frown deepen.

'I'm surprised you bothered to come back.' When she looked puzzled he said curtly, 'Don't pretend you didn't see me this afternoon—you were at Winters' place. I take it from the fond embrace I witnessed that you fell for whatever it was he told you.'

She turned away, but not before he saw the sheen of tears in her eyes. She was bundled unceremoniously back into the hall, Jago's body following her as he slammed the door behind him.

'Tears?'

'I got shampoo in my eyes,' she lied angrily. 'Will you please go away—I've got to get changed.' She opened the front door pointedly, turning her face away as he strode through it and disappeared into his car.

When he had gone she felt even more restless. She dried her hair, trying to concentrate on some work she had brought home, but her mind kept returning to Jago. Where had he been going? Out somewhere, that had been obvious, but who with? Her heart seemed to contract with pain as she thought of him with another woman, and on a shudder of realisation she acknowledged what she had been trying to keep at bay ever since he had swept into her life.

She had fallen in love with Jago Marsh. Right from the start she had fought against it, but she had not been able to stamp out the feelings he aroused within her. Panic swept through her. She couldn't have been so foolish— but she had!

Whatever happened Jago must not discover how she felt, she told herself fiercely. If he did he would manipulate her feelings quite ruthlessly until she was compelled to give in to her desire for him. That she would find heaven in his arms she no longer tried to deny, but it would be for a very brief spell, leaving her in the depths of hell when he no longer wanted her.

A knock on the door roused her. Frowning, she walked into the hall, glancing at the clock. It was half-past eight and she could think of no one who could call on her at this time on a Saturday evening. Despite herself a shiver ran over her as she remembered how remote the house was, and as she opened the door she reached for the safety chain, but she was too late. The person on the other side was already forcing the door back.

'Jago!' She stared up at him, unable to believe her eyes. 'What . . . What are you doing here?'

'I could ask you the same question,' he said grimly,

taking in her jeans and jumper. 'What happened? Or can I guess?'

It seemed pointless to lie any more, so she said calmly, 'As you so rightly said, David would rather spend his free time with Angie Townley.'

She had turned her back to him, not trusting herself to remain cool and indifferent if she had to look at him, but the silence between them made the hair on the back of her neck prickle warningly, and she swung round suddenly, her eyes defiant.

'Well, go on, tell me that you warned me! Tell me that you said all along that he didn't want me; that no man could ever want someone like me, that . . .'

Her composure broke and she tried to push past him, not wanting him to guess what had happened, but he moved forward, his body taking her full weight so that she was crushed against the muscled wall of his chest, his hands grasping her shoulders.

'Don't touch me!' she cried, shaking herself free, her whole body trembling. For one wild moment she had wanted to place her head on his shoulder and feel his knowing hands caress her into the awareness only he could arouse.

'Go and get changed,' he told her curtly. 'You're coming with me. If you refuse,' he added, anticipating her, 'I shall stay here with you. I'm not leaving you here on your own in this state. Winters ought to be thrashed for . . .'

'It isn't David's fault,' Storm began quickly, falling back when she saw the anger burning up under his skin, his eyes almost opaquely brilliant with the force of it.

'I don't believe it!' he breathed savagely. 'Even now, knowing what he is, you still defend him! What kind of masochist are you? What sort of woman are you? Go and get changed, Storm,' he said tiredly. 'And if you aren't back down here in half an hour, I'll come up and strip you myself.'

There was no doubting that he meant it.

Why had he come back? Had he sensed that she had been lying about David and returned to crow over her? The thought hurt.

She picked a dress from her wardrobe at random; it was plain black crêpe, hugging her throat at the front with long tight sleeves finishing at the wrist, the pencil-slim skirt emphasising her slender hips and legs. Viewed from the front the dress was starkly plain, almost puritan, but when she turned it was slashed down to her waist at the back the neck band fastening under her hair, her smooth silky skin a stark contrast to the mat black fabric.

She had only worn the dress once before, and seeing it on now, with new eyes, she almost took it off again. Ian had gone with her to buy it, telling her appreciatively that it was sexy, a comment which she had dismissed as brotherly teasing, but now she was not so sure. Against the black fabric her hair looked more red than brown, her eyes huge and dark in the pale oval of her face.

'Storm?'

The voice warned her that she was running out of time. Picking up her fur, she slipped on a pair of black heelless sandals and pulled open her bedroom door.

Jago watched her walk downstairs, his expression unreadable.

'I . . . I hope I'm not overdressed,' she said nervously when she reached him, her eyes on his frilled shirt.

'As far as I'm concerned, you're always overdressed, Storm,' he told her softly, taking her jacket from nerveless fingers and sliding it on to her shoulders. As his fingers brushed her skin, she trembled and in the mirror she saw his mouth tighten.

'Where are we going?' she asked.

'To see some friends of mine. Don't worry, you'll be quite safe,' he told her urbanely as he opened the door. 'They're a very respectably and happily married couple.

Tony is an old friend, I was best man at their wedding, and Valeria will be a very adequate chaperone.'

'Won't they think it strange when you turn up with me?' Storm asked nervously.

'They're quite accustomed to me doing strange things,' she was assured dryly, as Jago opened the car door for her. 'But if it puts your mind at rest there'll be such a crowd there that one more will hardly be noticed. Tony is one of the friends I was telling you about who's going to invest in the station.'

'Has he invested in your London station?' Storm asked. The dark interior of the car was creating a subtle intimacy she would have preferred to do without.

'No, I own that outright. No, Tony and I met at Cambridge.'

Cambridge? In the darkness Storm frowned. It must have been quite an achievement for a boy with Jago's background to win a place there.

'Mary Simmonds told me that you were brought up in a children's home,' she said impulsively. 'No wonder you want to help these children so much, it must have been dreadful . . .'

'Don't waste your pity on me,' Jago told her in a hard voice. 'My parents died while I was too young to remember them—a road accident—and there are worse places to grow up. Life's what you make of it, Storm. No one gets anywhere waiting for it to come to them. I'm not one of your lame dogs and I don't want your pity.'

His words hurt and she wished she had not agreed to accompany him. The evening stretched interminably ahead of her. How on earth would she cope thrown into a circle of complete strangers, who would probably all wonder what on earth a man like Jago was doing with a country mouse like her? No doubt she didn't compare at all favourably with his usual female companions—models, actresses, Society types.

Jago's friends lived in Chelsea, and Storm's eyes widened apprehensively as he stopped outside an elegant Regency terrace. Lights seemed to blaze from every window, elegant and expensive cars were parked outside, and Storm shivered as Jago escorted her up the stone steps and past the bay trees standing either side of the front door.

'De rigueur in Chelsea,' Jago told her, following her eyes.

The door opened and a diminutive blonde flung her arms round his neck and kissed him enthusiastically.

'Jago darling! We thought you weren't going to make it. Tony,' she called over her shoulder, 'Jago's here!'

Five minutes later Storm was being taken upstairs by her hostess, who as Jago had prophesied took her appearance in her stride.

'So you're the Storm Jago has been telling Tony about,' she said as she opened a bedroom door. 'Just leave your jacket there and then I'll take you downstairs and introduce you around. I'm afraid you'll probably find you've already lost Jago,' she said, wrinkling her nose. 'When he and Tony get together there's no stopping them. I hope you aren't the jealous type,' she added as they went back downstairs. 'Although I'm sure you've nothing to worry about. Jago isn't easily swayed once he's made up his mind about something.'

'I don't think you understand,' Storm said anxiously. 'There's nothing romantic between us . . .'

Valeria turned to stare at her, her pretty, intelligent brown eyes openly amazed.

'My dear, you can't be for real?' she said breathlessly. 'But don't worry, your secret's safe with me.'

She was in no state to argue with her kindly hostess, Storm decided. Let Jago explain the position to her, after all they were his friends.

True to her promise Valeria took her round and introduced her to several people. A young man with fair hair and blue eyes, whom Storm vaguely recognised from television, made a big thing of fetching her a drink and getting her something to eat. Storm searched discreetly for Jago and saw him standing to one side talking to a short auburn-haired man who she guessed must be their host.

Her blond companion introduced himself as Richard Kingsley, and although the name meant nothing to Storm, she sensed that it was supposed to.

Pop music blared from a stereo in one corner of the room and several couples gyrated on the floor.

So these were the 'beautiful people', Storm thought wryly. A tall black-haired girl walked up to Jago, putting her hand on his arm as she whispered something in his ear, and Storm wasn't surprised to see the two of them dancing together.

When Richard suggested that they join them she shook her head, but he grabbed her arm, tugging her towards him, and rather than make a scene she gave in.

He was an expert dancer, although a little flamboyant, and she knew they were attracting attention from the others. When the music changed tempo to a slow, dreamy number, she was pleased at first, until under cover of the darkness, Richard's hands caressed her back, his breath whisky-flavoured as he murmured softly, 'Mm—sexy, and you've got lovely skin. How about we split and go off somewhere on our own, like my place?'

Storm pushed him away.

'Thanks, but no, thanks,' she told him coolly.

'What's the matter with you?' he objected, pulling her against him. 'Relax!'

'She isn't in your league, Rich,' Jago drawled at her shoulder. 'And besides, she's with me. Be a good boy and go and find someone else to play with, mm?'

Storm didn't know whether to be glad or sorry when Richard released her.

'The mighty Jago Marsh snaps his fingers and everyone falls into line,' she said bleakly when they were alone.

'Don't tell me you were enjoying it,' Jago taunted. 'Because if you were you have a funny way of showing it.'

'I'm surprised you noticed. You looked pretty well occupied yourself!'

'Janice is an old friend,' was all he said, but Storm didn't like the way his eyes narrowed.

'Storm, Jago, there you are,' Valeria said breathlessly. 'Why aren't you dancing? Dance with her, Jago,' she urged. 'That's what parties are for.'

'I don't want to . . .' Storm began, but it was too late. Jago's arms were sliding over her shoulders to clasp her waist, her body propelled forward until it rested against his, as her hands linked behind his head.

'Try to look as though you're enjoying it,' he whispered, his breath sending shivers over her exposed skin, 'otherwise you'll ruin my reputation!'

Beneath his jacket she could feel his muscles, the pressure of his hands keeping her against him. It would be fatally easy to relax against him and give him the victory she knew he was determined to have, but it was too dangerous.

She was glad when the music ended, and the wry smile Jago gave her told her that he was aware of her relief. His eyes lingered on the firm swell of her breasts and she knew it was deliberate punishment when he said softly to Valeria. 'Time we weren't here, I think. Say goodnight to Tony for me.'

'If you wait a minute I'll go and find him,' Valeria began, laughing when she saw his face. 'Ah, like that, is it?' she asked with a knowing look at Storm. 'I'll go and get your coat, then, although something tells me you aren't going to need it.'

'Did you have to do that?' Storm asked, close to tears, when she had gone. 'It was obvious what she thought.'

'Like I just said,' Jago said lazily, 'I've got my reputation to think of.' He smiled wickedly at her as Valeria returned with her jacket, kissing the other woman on the cheek and promising to be in touch.

'Enjoy yourself?' he asked when they were out of the city.

'It was better than staying at home by myself, brooding,' Storm admitted. 'You were right about what you said about David.' There was a lump in her throat and it hurt to speak, but it had to be said. 'I don't think he ever cared for me at all.'

She felt rather than saw the sideways flick of his eyes and prayed that he wouldn't say anything. She was tired and leaned back in her seat, closing her eyes, as she tried to blot out the sight of the man next to her.

She must have fallen asleep, for the next thing she knew was a sudden rush of cold air and the reassuring thump of something against her ear. She struggled through the layers of tiredness and heard Jago whisper in her ear, 'It's okay. You fell asleep in the car. Which is your room?'

'You're not carrying me upstairs!' she protested, panic feathering across her skin. 'I can manage on my own.'

He must have taken her key from her pocket, and she cursed herself for falling asleep. The fabric of his jacket felt rough on the exposed flesh of her back, and she felt his muscles stiffen as he ignored her words.

It wasn't difficult for him to guess which room was hers. She had left the light on. Jago dropped her gently on her bed, his hands either side of her on the coverlet, imprisoning her against it.

'You have lovely skin,' he told her softly, dropping down beside her, his hand feathering a caress up her neck.

Shock trembled through her, and as though in a trance she watched the slow downward descent of his head, his lips silky against her throat, teasing and tantalising until she was breathing unevenly, her hands clenched desperately at her sides to prevent them sliding round him. He had removed his jacket and his shirt glimmered palely in the dark.

This gentle, almost tender assault upon her senses was far harder to withstand than any violence, and as his hands caressed the bare skin of her throat desire flamed through her. Barely aware of what she was doing, she slid her hands feverishly upwards, tracing the bones of his shoulders, her neck arching as his lips tormented her heated skin. Her hands trembled over the buttons of his shirt, sliding inside to caress the warmth of his flesh.

His low groan startled her, and her eyes widened as she felt him release the top of her dress, and then before she could protest the hair-roughened warmth of his chest was crushing her breasts, his breathing quickened as she was moulded against him, her bones turning to water at the touch of his body against hers.

His mouth teased and tasted, beginning a long slow arousal, that drove her mindless with aching longing. When her dress slithered to the floor and Jago raised himself slightly to look slowly along the length of her body, she felt only quickening excitement; her arms reached for him, her mouth parting eagerly as he kissed her. His hands tangled in her hair, and when he lifted his head he was breathing heavily.

'You're beautiful, do you know that?' he said softly, bending his head to find the valley between her breasts, his lips deliberately provocative as they caressed the silky swelling flesh, and Storm trembled against him as his mouth finally closed over the nipple, sensation exploding inside her as she arched instinctively, moaning softly as her body demanded his complete possession.

'Say it, Storm,' he urged softly before claiming her mouth. 'Tell me you want me. Forget Winters . . .'

It was like an injection of ice into her veins. Oh, how could she be so stupid? She pulled away from him, her eyes bitter in the darkness.

'Get out!' she snapped at him. 'Get out of here! I hate you!'

She turned away, closing her eyes, refusing to look at him as he stood up.

His fingers grasped her chin, forcing her to meet his eyes. 'It's okay, I'm going,' he said wryly. 'I guess my timing was at fault. You shouldn't have worn that damned dress. The thought of how little you were wearing underneath it's been driving me crazy damned near all night. I'm not totally without feelings, Storm. You've taken a hard knock over Winters, but that doesn't make me any less determined. You've proved tonight that you're not exactly indifferent to me. And I'm one hell of a long way from being indifferent to you. I'm prepared to give you some time, so I won't press matters to their logical conclusion tonight—although we both know that I could.' His hands cupped her face so that it was impossible for her to look away, although she felt the heat sear her skin as his eyes lingered on her body.

'If I don't go now, I'll end up spending the night with you whether you want it or not,' he said at last. 'I haven't forgotten that vow I made to hear you say you want me, Storm, and it still holds good. Now kiss me and I'll go.'

She was trembling all over, but she still raised her mouth to his, her fingers curling into the thickness of his hair as her tongue traced the outline of his lips, feeling them harden under the tentative caress.

As his mouth took possession of hers her hands slid on to his shoulders, the muscles contracting beneath her touch.

'Forget Winters,' he told her jerkily as he released her. 'Forget him, Storm.'

Long after he had gone she lay wakeful and anguished. Her body throbbed with an unappeased ache and to her shame she acknowledged that if he had decided to stay with her she could not have refused him.

It was just as she feared. In love she was desperately at risk, wanting to yield her mind and her body. She closed her eyes, trying to relax into sleep.

There was no way now that she was ever going to persuade Jago that she was indifferent to him. All she could hope to do was to prevent him from discovering the depth of her love.

For a moment she let herself dwell on how it would feel to have Jago return her love, but she quickly dismissed the thought, knowing it to be impossible.

In some ways she almost wished he had stayed with her. Once he had taken what he had wanted he would surely lose interest, and already she was waiting for the pain she knew would follow their lovemaking as surely as night must follow day.

Work kept her busy for most of the following week. Because she had her father's car she told Jago that there was no need for him to give her a lift. As it happened he was tied up in meetings during the week, and she saw very little of him. He rang her every night at eleven o'clock to check that everything was all right as he had promised her parents.

One evening before he rang off he reminded her that Saturday was the evening fixed for the housewarming-cum-business get-together he had organised.

Rather reluctantly Storm asked if there was anything she could do to help, but he told her that everything was in hand.

'I intend to find a housekeeper after Christmas,' he told her, reinforcing her impression that he intended to make his Cotswold house his permanent home. 'But for Saturday I've organised some outside caterers. We've used them before in London and they're pretty good.'

She sometimes forgot that he had another life far removed from that at Radio Wyechester, Storm reflected as she hung up. The evening he took her to visit his friends had been a sample of that life—moneyed, sophisticated, a far cry from the quiet country existence she enjoyed.

She guessed that Tony and Valeria would be among the business associates Jago had invited. As one of the backers of Radio Wyechester Tony would want to inspect the team. In her heart of hearts she didn't want to go to the party, but she knew that to refuse would only cause comment.

There hadn't been a whisper of David's defection at the studio, but she knew that the others must be aware of what had happened. She herself had seen David in Wyechester with Angie Townley clinging to his arm, and she wondered if Jago had primed them to keep silent.

To her surprise he had not made any attempt to follow up the advantage David's departure had given him. At first Storm thought this was due to pressure of business, because the week had been very hectic, but then she started to wonder if Jago now considered that without David to use as a barrier, her capitulation was only a matter of time. He knew well enough how he affected her; he was far too experienced not to appreciate her reaction to him. That episode in her bedroom had been a complete giveaway; a moment of weakness which must not be allowed to happen again. Because Storm was still determined that she would not give in.

She had had ample time to think the whole thing through. Jago did not love her, he merely wanted her, and she was honest enough to know that as far as she was concerned, desire would never be enough. In fact she suspected that to give in now and allow him to possess her completely would only increase her need for him.

The initial response to the search for foster-parents had been even better than they had hoped. With the aid of the local Social Services Department a formula had been arranged for dealing with the prospective 'parents', and already the Matron of the home had high hopes that some of the younger children were going to find loving homes.

'The older kids are a tough bunch,' Pete told her as they discussed the progress of the scheme. They were sitting in the studio surrounded by all the equipment, drinking mugs of coffee, while Mike hosted the late morning show.

'But their stories would melt perma-frost. I want to try and get a couple of them on the show so that they can put their side of things; what they're looking for in a family, that sort of thing.'

'Sounds a good idea, but you'll have to get Jago's approval,' Storm warned him. Released from David's carping disapproval, Pete had blossomed into a hard-working enthusiast, putting them all to shame with the work he was putting in on their various projects.

As well as offers to act as foster-parents, the appeal had brought a positive avalanche of free gifts, tickets and invitations for the children, and she had taken on the extra duties of sorting these out.

No one could deny that there was a far more optimistic atmosphere in the studios these days Storm admitted. One of the first things Sam Townley had done following his defection had been to put up their rent, but Jago was making plans to find them fresh accommodation.

'He's talking about starting right from scratch,' Pete told her enthusiastically. 'Brand new equipment, the whole bit. Apparently he was quite taken with Harmers' place. That's one of the reasons he's gone up to London today, to have talks with some architects.'

This was news to Storm, and she bent over her coffee mug, hiding her face.

It was no use trying to convince herself that Jago's interest could ever be anything than merely physical, and to be fair to him he had never suggested that it might. It was only her imagination that kept tormenting her with images of what might have been had he returned her feelings. Which was all so much nonsense, she told herself feelingly as she drove home, because Jago Marsh was most emphatically not the tame, domestic type.

Her father's daily paper was lying on the mat behind the front door when Storm unlocked it. She hadn't bothered cancelling it, and she glanced through it while she had her tea.

Jago's familiar features stared back at her from the centre pages, sending disturbing sensations cramping through her stomach. The photograph was accompanied by an article describing his involvement with Radio Wyechester, and the reporter had obviously questioned him about his future role with the station when combined with his other business interests.

His reply was determinedly noncommittal. As he pointed out to the reporter, he had run City Radio, his London station, for five years, during which time it had crept steadily up the ratings charts until it reached the top, where it had remained for close on two years. With his management team all hand-picked the station no longer needed his constant attention, so it was plainly time to turn his sights in other directions.

The reporter had mentioned the offers he had received from the States, and Storm's stomach lurched protestingly at the thought of the width of the Atlantic between them. Again Jago had been circumspect in his response, but there was nothing to reassure her in his claim that one must take life as it came, living each day as it happened.

A man of his drive and ambition wouldn't be satisfied with a small station like theirs for very long, she admitted miserably, folding the paper. She had perhaps twelve months before he went out of her life altogether. And she didn't know whether to be glad or sorry. Twelve months was a long time to hold him at bay—always supposing he didn't lose interest and grow bored with her. But on the other hand, it was far too fleeting to allow her to gather enough memories to last through the long, love-starved years to come.

Saturday was also Storm's birthday, and she woke up in the morning feeling rather downcast.

The postman had been by the time she was washed and dressed, but apart from a handful of cards from friends, there was nothing for her.

In the past both Ian and John had remembered her birthdays with lavish gifts, and although she could understand that her elder brother was probably far too busy to remember the date, let alone buy a present, she was disappointed that there wasn't something from Ian. A long, newsy letter would have helped to alleviate the despondency creeping over her.

It was just as well her mother couldn't see her, she admitted wryly, pulling a face at her own reflection as she walked through the hall.

She couldn't stay miserable all day just because her family appeared to have forgotten her, and she was in her room changing into a clean pair of cords when the phone rang. The nearest extension was the one in her parents' bedroom, and she hurried to answer it, pulling a soft pale grey angora sweater on as she did so.

'Storm?' The sound of her mother's voice almost brought tears to her eyes. 'Happy birthday, darling. Is David taking you somewhere nice this evening?'

'It's Jago's party, Mum,' Storm replied, glad that she had no need to explain exactly why she wasn't going out with David. Her excuse seemed to satisfy Mrs Templeton, for she said happily, 'Of course—I'd forgotten.'

The call was only a short one—there was barely time for Storm to do more than say 'hello' to everyone, including her sister-in-law-to-be—but when she hung up she was feeling considerably less lonely.

Back in her room she slicked lip gloss over her lips, and brushed her hair. Mrs Jennings, her mother's 'daily', did not come at weekends, and by the time she had cleaned away her breakfast things and tidied up it was nearly lunchtime.

She was just debating about whether to bother with a meal when the front door bell pealed. When she opened it, Jago was standing there. Dark cords hugged his lean hips and long, muscular legs, a soft shirt open at the neck to reveal the tanned warmth of his chest, a leather jacket slung carelessly over one shoulder as his eyes slid appreciatively over the soft curves beneath her sweater, and the slender length of her legs in their damson cords.

'Hello.' It was an effort to drag her eyes away from him, and she veiled them quickly with her lashes, hoping she hadn't betrayed the hunger he aroused in her. His Ferrari was parked in the drive and she wondered why he had called.

'Not going to invite me in?' he asked softly.

A crazy nervousness was spiralling up inside her, her mouth dry as her pulses pounded out their urgent message. As Jago walked past her, his eyes lingered on her mouth, and the sensual scrutiny increased her inner tension.

'I was just going to have lunch.'

'Then I'm just in time,' he said smoothly, the comment betraying her into lifting surprised eyes to his face.

'You're having lunch with me,' he told her, as though she had no say in the matter. 'A birthday treat.' His mouth twisted sardonically before she could refuse. 'Call it a form of recompense for depriving you of Winters' company. Had it not been for me no doubt you would have spent the day with him.' His eyes dropped to her hand, his fingers grasping it, running lightly along the knuckles, his expression unfathomable. 'Who knows, perhaps he might even have given you a ring.'

Something in his satirical expression caused a shaft of pain so intense that she almost gasped out loud, snatching her fingers away.

'I don't think so,' she replied in a low voice. 'David never loved me, I know that now . . .'

'And I'm the cruel bastard who forced the knowledge on you, is that it? Get your coat, Storm. I've booked us a table for one.'

'Without asking me?' Storm demanded. He was treating her like a Dutch uncle and she wasn't sure if she liked it. The intense excitement she had experienced when she saw him standing outside the door had given way to increased depression, a vague aching in her temples warning her of a latent headache.

'Without asking you,' Jago agreed urbanely. 'But you're coming with me if I have to bundle you into the car myself. And don't bother telling me that no company is preferable to mine—your expression when you opened the door was very illuminating,' he concluded dryly.

She was glad of the excuse of fetching her coat, for it meant that she could turn away from him to hide her confusion. She had a very good idea of how she had looked when she opened the door, and if he hadn't guessed how she felt about him by now, he was not the man she thought.

He had booked a table for them at a well-known and extremely exclusive country club several miles away, and Storm sat silently at his side as the powerful car responded to his touch.

Several days' frost had turned the earth to iron, a pale lemon sun struggling through the layers of dove grey cloud. The air was very still, the countryside held fast in the grip of an early winter.

What was he thinking? Storm wondered, darting a look at her companion. His profile told her nothing, his lean hands controlling the car, with much the same ease that they controlled her, she thought unhappily, and yet she knew that she ached to feel them upon her again, and that if he were to stop the car now and turn to her, she would be powerless to deny him whatever he wanted. And even that was an understatement. There was nothing passive about the way she felt about him. He changed gear, the movement tautening the muscles of his thighs, and she longed to reach out and touch him. Heated colour burned along her cheekbones and she dragged her eyes away, forcing herself to focus on the scenery outside the car instead of the man within.

The country club was a low Cotswold stone building set in gardens which in summer were a blaze of colour. They were shown to a table in a window alcove, the head waiter flourishing a menu the moment they were sitting down.

Storm was sure she wouldn't be able to eat a thing, but a delicious fresh Florida cocktail restored her appetite for the duck which the head water had recommended, and the wine which Jago had chosen helped her tensed muscles to relax. In point of fact, she felt amost lightheaded. During their first course she had drunk her wine quite quickly, trying to dispel her nervousness, and the waiter had insisted on topping up her glass, so that she had consumed far more than she usually drank.

Jago refused a sweet in favour of cheese and biscuits, and Storm allowed herself to be persuaded into a rich chocolate and whipped cream confection, which she pushed round her plate, unable to lift her eyes from Jago's hands as he cut a wedge of cheese.

A cup of coffee helped to reduce the cottonwoolly feeling which had engulfed her, but she made no demur when Jago slid his arm along her shoulders as they left the club.

Outside the clouds had obliterated the sun, and it was cold, the afternoon, already fading to an early dusk. Storm shivered, despite her fur jacket, and Jago pulled her against him, her senses immediately taking fire from the brief contact.

'I'll come and collect you tonight,' he told her as he

opened the car door. 'About eight?'

'I can walk,' Storm demurred, but he shook his head, sliding into his own seat and switching on the engine.

'It's too far.'

'Will Tony and Valeria be there?'

He nodded. 'Mm. Tony was quite taken with you, but I've told him you're all mine.' He laughed softly when he saw her expression. 'As far as employment goes, of course. You're contracted to Wyechester, and I don't intend to let him entice you away with promises of fame and fortune in television.'

'You don't have a very high opinion of female loyalty, do you?' Storm asked him. 'I heard you lecture once, and you were very scathing about women in the media.'

She felt him turn to look at her, and could not meet his narrowed scrutiny.

'Is that what all the defiance was about? Don't pretend you don't know what I mean. It was plain from the moment I walked into the studios that you had it in for me. I thought it was purely on account of Winters . . .'

'I didn't like your attitude towards women in radio,' Storm admitted, 'Nor the implication that they were merely using it as a stepping stone to television. We aren't all blinded by the glamour of the small screen. Personally I find radio work far less restricting, with much greater scope . . .'

'I was generalising,' Jago told her. 'And in general terms my comments still hold good. Lots of girls do join local radio stations with their eyes on television channels.'

'Will there be many people from City Radio there tonight?' Storm asked curiously. So far Jago seemed to be keeping the two sides of his life in completely separate compartments, and she wondered if this was by design.

'One or two,' he replied unhelpfully, as he turned off the main road and down a narrow country lane which Storm knew led to his own house.

'I want to go straight home,' she protested.

Jago laughed. 'Relax, I don't intend to exact payment for your lunch, if that's what's worrying you.' His mouth twisted slightly. 'Who are you fighting, Storm, me—or yourself?'

Before she could answer they had come to rest in front of the house. Storm had never been inside it before, and glanced around her with interest.

'Does it have your approval?' Jago mocked. They were standing in a large square hallway with a polished wooden floor, rising up one side to an overhanging balcony. The room had an air of space and light and the decor was cool and simple.

Jago pushed open a door and Storm stepped inside a huge lounge furnished with two large settees covered in off-white fabric, her feet sinking into a deep pile carpet in a soft shade of green. Green and cream curtains with a hint of peach hung against the windows, and deep rust-coloured lamps echoed the colour scheme. It was very luxurious and no doubt very expensive, and just the sort of room she would have expected in such a modern house.

'It was decorated like this when I bought it,' Jago told her indifferently, motioning her to one of the settees. 'It suits me for the moment.'

In view of his lack of interest in the decor Storm wondered why he had bought such a large house, when he would have had an apartment in Wyechester itself, which would surely have been more convenient. She stole a look at his face, wondering if the house represented some subconscious childhood urge for a family home. The subject was too personal for her to broach and instead she studied one of the modern abstracts hanging on the wall, wondering what the rest of the house was like.

'Would you like something to drink?' Jago asked her abruptly. She shook her head. She had a feeling that she had already had too much. That wine with her lunch had been a mistake.

'Stay here a minute,' he told her, disappearing and leaving her alone. Why had he brought her here? To exact the admission he had told her she would eventually give?

She didn't hear him come back; the thick carpet muffled his footsteps, and when his fingers grasped her chin, she started nervously, her tongue wetting her upper lip, a startled gasp escaping her as Jago's hands slid into her hair, tilting her head back, his own tongue stroking her lips with a sensual expertise that had her shuddering achingly against him, as his mouth closed on hers.

After what seemed like aeons, she came back to earth, too bemused to care what he might read in her unguarded expression as her eyes reflected her reaction to his kisses.

'Happy birthday,' he murmured softly, against her lips. 'Now turn round.'

Obediently she did as she was bid, and a startled cry broke from her lips as she saw the small pile of presents on the coffee table. Too surprised to disguise her pleasure, she exclaimed shakily, 'For me?'

'Your parents didn't want you to think they'd forgotten you.'

There were half a dozen prettily wrapped parcels. Storm opened the two smallest first, gasping with delight when she saw the delicate gold chain and matching bracelet that her parents had bought for her.

'Here, let me,' Jago offered as she struggled with the clasp. The touch of his fingers on her skin sent shivers running down her spine and when they lingered for a second she held her breath, her bones melting to water at the memory of the delight they could evoke.

'It's fastened now,' he told her coolly, giving her a little push. 'Open the rest.'

There was a beautiful silk scarf from Andrea and a

letter which she put aside until later, and a small square parcel from John which contained her favourite Chanel perfume.

'He knows how much I like it,' she explained, puzzled by the expression on Jago's face as she picked up the last box, a large square package, tied with pretty pink and silver ribbons and wrapped in pink and grey paper.

When she had removed the wrappings she stared in amazement, searching for a card to say who the gift was from. An elegant white box held her favourite Chanel toiletries, and she exclaimed delightedly when she saw a large bottle of bath oil, wondering who could have bought her such an expensive present.

'There isn't a card,' Jago drawled urbanely above her. 'I thought you'd be able to guess the sentiments expressed easily enough.'

Storm stared up at him. 'You mean this is from you?' She could hardly believe it. 'But . . .'

'I noticed you were wearing it the other night,' Jago cut across her protests, 'and I thought you would find it more acceptable than something more intimate.'

More intimate! Her senses reeled. Tonight she would attend his party, her body, whose contours he already knew intimately, softened and perfumed with his gift.

'You shouldn't have . . .' she began in a husky whisper, standing up unsteadily.

'But I did, and now you can thank me,' Jago murmured silkily, taking her in his arms.

His mouth was warm and firm and she made no demur when his hands slid under her sweater caressing her spine before curving upwards to cup her breasts. When he released her she was breathing jerkily and he held her away from him for a few seconds, studying her unprotected face.

'Now try and tell me that you don't want me,' he said evenly.

She couldn't, of course, and she gathered up her presents in numb misery.

For a moment in his arms she had forgotten that all this was just a game and allowed herself to believe. . . . What? That he might eventually come to care for her?

She sat in silence as he drove her home, wishing she could find some excuse to miss the party. Her heart had started to ache in earnest, a legacy of the wine at lunchtime and her see-sawing emotions, she suspected.

As he helped her out of the car Jago bent over her, his eyes hard.

'Don't start searching for excuses not to come tonight Storm,' he warned. 'You're coming if I have to drag you screaming all the way!'

Under the words Storm read a meaning of a different kind, an implicit reminder of his intentions, and she trembled with the knowledge that should he choose to assert his power over her, there was little she would be able to do to deny him.

CHAPTER NINE

SHE had never dreamed that her mother would entrust her birthday presents to Jago, Storm reflected as she prepared for the party. In fact she wished that she had not done so. There was little doubt in her mind that this was why he had bought her something himself, but the lavishness of the gift dismayed her. She had told herself she wouldn't use it, but the temptation had proved too great and the fragrance of the bath oil hung on the air, enveloping her in a sensual perfumed cloud.

She was wearing her new dress, and added a touch of blusher to her cheekbones to hide the pallor of her skin. Jago arrived just as she was adding her lip gloss, and she tried to stem the weakness rising in her as his eyes slid over her body with blatant meaning.

'Sexy and yet subtley virginal,' he pronounced when the inspection was over, adding obliquely, 'It suits you.'

Her perfume filled the interior of the car, and Storm stiffened, half expecting him to make some comment. Jago himself was wearing hip-hugging dark pants, a silky white shirt open at the neck under his sheepskin jacket. As they drove under the street lights Storm saw the faint beading of moisture at his throat, her breathing suddenly restricted, her hands clenched at her side to prevent her from leaning across and touching his clean, damp skin with her lips.

It was madness to feel like this, she warned herself, but she could do nothing to stop her pulses racing when he helped her out of the car. Almost day by day her aching need of him increased. The touch of his hand, initially no more than an intimacy to be avoided, now burned and tormented, inciting her flesh to demand more.

The first people Storm recognised as she entered the crowded living room were Tony and Valeria, obviously very much at home among a crowd whom Storm did not recognise but guessed must be friends of Jago's from London. As Jago took her jacket, a tall blonde girl detached herself from the throng swaying seductively across the room to pout provocatively at Jago as she placed plum-tipped fingers on his arm.

'Jago darling,' she murmured breathlessly, 'where have you been? I've missed you. I want to hear all about this darling little station you've bought. Come and talk to me.'

Her eyes rested disparagingly on Storm's set face, before she curved her body against Jago's arm, neatly excluding Storm from the conversation. On any other occasion she would have been amused by the other girl's manoeuvres, but where Jago was concerned, she acknowledged unhappily, she was too emotionally involved to feel anything but intense, searing jealousy.

'Madeleine, I know she's only small, but there's no need to crush Storm underfoot,' Jago drawled dryly, forcing the blonde to acknowledge her presence.

No doubt he was quite used to these confrontations between his female companions, Storm thought bitterly, and probably even derived a certain wry amusement from them.

Madeleine acknowledged her with a voice that dripped condescension, her eyes dismissing Storm as an unworthy opponent as she immediately launched into a conversation featuring mutual friends in London whose names meant nothing to Storm, apart from the fact that she had occasionally come across them in the gossip columns. In the opposite corner of the room she could see Pete chatting to Tony, and excusing herself, she went over to join them, glad to escape from Madeleine's chilling glances.

'Jago's got a great place here,' Pete commented enviously when Storm joined them, and she could see from his
expression that he was thinking of the day when he would
be successful enough to own something as luxurious.

'It is lovely,' Valeria agreed, smiling warmly at Storm.
'A lot of our friends were surprised when he gave up his
London service flat to move down here, but I wasn't.'

She said it so confidently that Storm looked enquiringly
at her. Jago was still talking to Madeleine, his dark head
bent over her blonde one. The pose was familiar to Storm
from gossip column glossies, and jealousy ate into her.

'Don't be fooled by the sophisticated exterior,' Valeria
warned her. 'Other people have dismissed Jago as nothing
more than an elegant playboy—to their cost. What he is
today he achieved single-handed, and you don't do that
without collecting a few scars on the way. Jago was an
orphan, you know,' she told Storm, who was a little surprised that as a friend of Jago's of such long standing,
Valeria should speak to her in this vein, but an explanation was soon forthcoming. Tony and Pete were deep in a
discussion on the rival merits of local and national radio,
and Valeria drew Storm a little to one side.

'Look, perhaps I'm sticking my nose in where it isn't
wanted,' she began without preamble, wrinkling the item
in question with a rueful air. 'Tony's always telling me
that I act before I think, but on this occasion intuition
tells me that I'm right. It's pretty obvious you aren't just
one of Jago's decorative idiots. Oh, you're pretty all right,'
she added hastily.

'But I'm not cast in the same mould as Madeleine, for
instance,' Storm supplied comprehendingly.

Valeria grinned. 'Would you honestly want to be? Oh,
I know she looks fantastic, but once you've said that
you've said the lot, and I'm not just being bitchy. I could
never understand what Jago saw in those empty-headed
model types he used to squire around—apart from the

obvious, of course. When he brought you to our house the other week, I was astonished, at first, and then when I'd had time to think about it—the fact that he joined Radio Wyechester so quickly, without a word to anyone, buying a house down here, the whole thing—I realised that this time it must be serious . . .'

Storm took a deep breath.

'I wish it was,' she said frankly, for some reason feeling that she could trust Valeria. 'But it isn't. At least not as far as Jago's concerned.'

There was a long silence, and then Valeria said briskly, 'If that means what I think it means, I've really gone and put my foot in it, haven't I? I could have sworn that Jago felt something for you, though. He looked definitely possessive the other night . . .'

'He does feel something for me,' Storm said quietly, glad of the opportunity to get it off her chest. 'He wants me—but nothing more.'

'I see . . .' There was compassion and understanding in Valeria's eyes. 'And has he . . .?'

Storm shook her head. 'Not yet.'

'But once he discovers how you feel about him, it's only going to be a matter of time?'

'Unless he gets tired of the game first,' Storm agreed with a wintry smile which she did little to disguise. 'I was a fool to come here tonight, but Jago insisted and somehow it seemed more sensible to give in.'

'Mm.' Valeria's eyes rested thoughtfully on her pale face. 'You're a lot braver than I would be in the same circumstances. Jago's a fool,' she added abruptly. 'You would be just right for him, Storm. You're just what he needs, and when I saw this house I felt sure he must be planning . . . I'm sorry,' she apologised, 'that was tactless of me.'

'Don't worry about it,' Storm replied gaily. 'It's just that you made me sound like a particularly nasty dose of medicine! Pete and Tony are looking a bit suspicious—I think we'd better rejoin them.'

Tony was an entertaining raconteur with a fund of stories relating to the early days of independent radio which had both Storm and Pete laughing. Once or twice her eyes strayed betrayingly to Jago, and Pete, watching her, remarked enviously, 'Who's that with Jago? She looks just my type.'

'Madeleine Rivers. She's a model-cum-actress who's been pestering the life out of Jago to use his influence to get her a T.V. part. She hosted a chat show on City Radio for a while, and she's done some hostessing for one of the smaller regional T.V. stations.'

Jago was looking down at the blonde, his expression cynically amused, and Storm was bleakly aware that Madeleine Rivers wouldn't hesitate to use her body, if she thought it might help advance her career. No wonder Jago was inclined to be contemptuous of her sex! No doubt if Madeleine had her way she would not be returning to London but spending the night here with Jago, preferably in his bed. Abruptly Storm turned away, unable to bear the pain knifing through her body.

'Dance?' Pete invited casually.

Storm nodded.

Their steps matched effortlessly. They often visited the local discos together, and Storm swayed to the music without having to think about moving, her body automatically adapting itself to the beat. Someone turned the lights down low, and the tempo changed. Pete's thin, wiry body pressed up against hers as they gyrated slowly together in time to the music.

Out of the corner of her eye Storm caught sight of Madeleine, clinging sexily to Jago's shoulders as her body moulded itself against him. Nausea churned in the pit of her stomach, the headache which had been threatening all day suddenly transforming into a throbbing pain, pounding in her temples.

'Are you okay?' Pete asked anxiously when she stumbled for the second time. 'Look, let me get you a drink.'

Storm tried to tell him that she didn't want one, but he insisted on her drinking the full tumbler of liquid he brought back with him. It burned her throat like fire, leaving a faint residue of taste that was vaguely familiar.

'Vodka,' Pete told her with a grin. 'Guaranteed to beat any headache!'

Storm gasped as the raw spirit hit her stomach, her eyes widening, as she realised that Pete had barely diluted it.

A Dr Hook tape echoed sexily round the room, the blatant message in the words causing Storm to tremble with the longing the words evoked, and search the darkness for Jago's dark head.

With a sick certainty she saw that he was missing, and so was Madeleine. So they hadn't even bothered to wait until everyone else had left. No doubt she didn't stubbornly claim to be in love with anyone else while his hands caressed her, and Storm knew that it would be Jago's name on her lips at the ultimate moment of possession.

Sickness crept over her. The Madeleines of this world were well suited to the Jagos—a mutual exchange of passion without the unnecessary complications of love. Storm bit her lip, suddenly convinced that she was going to be sick, and stumbled out of the room on legs that suddenly refused to support her.

A dim light illuminated the square hall and she pushed open the first door, which proved to be a study. The room was in darkness and at first she thought it unoccupied, and then she heard the unmistakable slither of fabric as someone moved. Her eyes pierced the darkness to find the leather chesterfield she hadn't noticed on entry, and, the blood stormed into her face as Madeleine's blonde head lifted from Jago's shoulder to eye her contemptuously, the girl's skin gleaming like the inside of a shell in the darkness.

'For God's sake, darling,' she drawled to Jago, 'I told you we should have gone upstairs. Now we've shocked your little advertising controller!'

As Storm stumbled through the door, she thought she heard Jago's voice, but whatever he said was drowned by Madeleine's tinkling laughter.

Closing the door silently behind her, Storm walked blindly into the kitchen. Sickness rose inside her, and she was unaware of Valeria calling her name, until the other woman touched her shoulder, her eyes concerned as she looked into her pale face.

'Storm, whatever's wrong?'

Not even to Valeria could she confide the scene she had unwittingly interrupted. Her tongue felt swollen and clumsy, her lips stiff as she tried to form words.

'It's only a headache,' she managed to mumble. 'I think I'll go home . . .'

'You can't!' Valeria protested. 'It's nearly a mile—Jago told me. Let me find him, he can drive you . . .'

'No!' The word was sharply painful, as her eyes clouded with the memory of Madeleine's exposed shoulders, her white arms twined round Jago's neck. 'No, there's no need. I'll be all right . . .'

'Well, you certainly aren't all right at the moment,' Valeria said roundly. 'Look, I've got some headache tablets with me. They're really good. Take a couple and go and lie down for a while. If you don't I shall go and find Jago,' she threatened.

Unwillingly Storm allowed herself to be persuaded upstairs to a bedroom luxuriously furnished in blues and greys, and yet somehow impersonal.

'Lie down,' Valeria commanded, disappearing into the en suite bathroom and returning with a glass of water and two pink capsules. 'Migraleve,' she explained when Storm looked at them doubtfully. 'They really are good. Just swallow them and have a sip of water, and then try to rest.'

'You won't tell anyone that I'm here?' Storm begged.

Valeria understood. 'I shan't tell a soul. Just stay here until you're feeling a bit better.'

The pills enveloped her in a hazy lassitude. She felt as though she were floating, she thought dreamily, as though somehow she had escaped the confines of her pain-racked body and were hovering above it. She moved restlessly, turning on to her side, her cheek pillowed against her hand, and let her thoughts drift as consciousness slowly left her.

Downstairs the party continued, but Storm was oblivious. She hadn't thought it necessary to tell Valeria about the large glass of vodka Pete had given her, and the alcohol combined with the strong tablets kept her deeply asleep.

She didn't know what woke her. At first she didn't realise where she was, and was confused by the odd angle of the moonlight through the window. Her headache had gone, but she was stiff. She slid off the bed, trying to find her shoes and accidentally knocking a book off the bedside cabinet. It fell to the floor with a thud and the bedroom door was suddenly thrust open, the light blinding her.

'What the . . . Storm?'

Jago was standing in the oblong of light, his hair tousled, his legs bare beneath the hem of his robe.

Storm stared at him, a bitter acid taste in her mouth. Had he and Madeleine decided to move upstairs after all?

'I'm sorry if I disturbed you,' she said stiffly. 'I fell asleep.'

'That I can see,' Jago agreed grimly. 'Have you any idea of the time?'

Storm wasn't wearing a watch. 'Is it late? I'd better go.

I'll go and say goodbye to Valeria and Tony.'

Jago laughed mirthlessly. 'You'll have a job—they left
hours ago. It's four o'clock in the morning, and the party
is well and truly over. I thought you'd gone. What the
devil are you doing in here?'

His anger crackled over her like ice. Her mouth felt dry
and she longed for a glass of water.

'I had a headache,' she whispered. 'I was going to go
home, but Valeria wouldn't let me. She wanted to fetch
you, and she gave me these tablets . . .'

Jago frowned suddenly and came farther into the room,
inspecting her heavy eyes and wan face.

'And you took them?' he asked incredulously. 'On top
of God only knows what you had to drink? Oh yes, I saw
Pete filling your glass . . .'

'I didn't know what it was,' Storm protested. 'I never
thought to tell Valeria. That must have been what made
me sleep so heavily.'

It was obvious from his rumpled hair and bare legs
that he had been in bed himself, and she wondered bitterly
if Madeleine was with him. It would be better if she never
found out.

'I'm sorry about this, but I'll go now,' she said hurriedly, slipping on her shoes. 'If you just tell me where my
coat is . . .'

'It's in my bedroom,' Jago told her succinctly, his eyes
never leaving her face. 'I thought you'd gone without it,
but you aren't going anywhere now. I'm damned if I'm
getting dressed to drive you half a mile down the road,
when you can stay here.'

'You don't need to take me,' Storm protested, 'I can
walk.'

'At four in the morning?' Jago's expression was ironic-
ally incredulous. 'Don't be a fool!' He switched on the
bedside lamp, bathing the room in a soft glow. 'This bed
isn't made up,' he told her, pulling back the cover in

confirmation of his words. 'You'd better sleep in mine. There's a spare quilt somewhere, I'll see if I can find it.'

'There's no need——' Storm began stiffly, but he overrode her protests, his expression impatient, as his fingers touched her bare skin, sending frissons of awareness surging through her.

'You're cold, and it will get a damned sight colder now the central heating's gone off. This room's only a guest room.'

'But I can't take your bed,' Storm protested weakly. 'I'll be quite all right here . . .'

'Please yourself,' Jago said curtly. 'I'll go and see if I can find that quilt.'

When he had gone Storm drew a shuddering breath. She was cold, but there was no way she could face the thought of sleeping in Jago's bed. At least Madeleine wasn't already in it, she thought hysterically.

There was an unpleasant taste in her mouth and she went into the bathroom to get a drink of water. It was tiled in toning shades of blue, and she shivered suddenly, feeling very cold. The towel rail was still warm and when she ran the water tentatively it was quite hot. The door had a lock and making sure it was closed Storm ran a hot bath, revelling in the feel of the water against her skin, bringing her back to life.

Wrapped in a large towel, she stepped into the bedroom. It was empty, and a quilt was heaped in the middle of the bed. Refusing to admit to any disappointment, she switched off the light, pulling the cover over her. Wrapped in its comforting warmth, sleep soon claimed her, but this time it was tormented by nameless fears; the nightmares of her childhood when unseen creatures stalked the darkness of some primaeval forest while she ran terrified from their stealthy pursuit. The forest closed in around her, her fear growing with each passing second, her tortured lungs strained to bursting point as she ran faster . . . faster . . .

'Storm!' She opened her eyes. Jago was frowning down at her, his hand on her shoulder. Her heart was racing, perspiration beading her forehead, the terrors of her nightmare still holding her in thrall. 'You screamed.'

'It was a nightmare—I'm sorry.' She knew she would not be able to get back to sleep. She rarely suffered from these nightmares now, but when they came they left her exhausted and nervous, starting at every shadow and far too strung up to close her eyes in case whatever it was that lurked so menacingly in the shadows emerged to claim her.

'You look like a child curled up there with your face all scrubbed clean and your hair ruffled. But you aren't a child, are you, Storm?' Jago muttered, as his arms slid round her his lips feathering soft kisses on her eyelids and nose.

'Jago, please!' Her voice shook and she raised her hands to hold him off, but the moment they came into contact with the firm hardness of his chest her fingers uncurled, moving convulsively over his muscles, a feverish pounding in her blood as she gave a faint moan.

'Don't fight it,' Jago advised her roughly, his hands sliding beneath the quilt to caress her frail shoulder bones, his eyes glittering as they probed the shadows. 'Kiss me, Storm,' he muttered hoarsely, his mouth forcing hers open as he teased her lips. And then his mouth possessed hers hotly, sweeping away her resistance as she clung to him. The quilt was flung aside, her body registering the fact that Jago had discarded his robe as he pulled her against him, making no secret of his desire. Moaning softly, Storm surrendered to the demand of his hands as they coaxed her into a wildly abandoned response, all conscious thought subordinated to the aching need spreading through her.

'Storm, you've been driving me crazy!' Jago murmured against her throat, his hands tangling in her hair as she arched convulsively beneath the sweeping sensation his lips aroused, her hands linking behind his head as he pushed the quilt aside, to study the frenzied passion of her body as it quivered softly beneath him.

Storm was beyond trying to hide how she felt. Her arms reached for him, her eyes blind with longing. As his hand moved slowly along her body, her breasts swelled and throbbed, a satisfied groan breaking from her lips as his mouth descended to their creamy fullness as he caressed first one and then the other with a slow sureness that drove her into his arms, with small, hoarse cries.

His lips returned to hers, no gentleness in their touch now, but Storm was beyond the need for gentleness, welcoming the fierce thrust of his body against her, as his thighs parted hers and the warm male scent of him filled her nostrils.

Jago was breathing hard, his breath rasping against her skin, leaving her in no doubt about his own arousal.

'Say it, Storm,' he muttered urgently as he trembled against her. 'Tell me you want me ... only me,' he demanded fiercely.

'I want you, Jago,' Storm muttered mindlessly, brutally jerked out of her dream when he grasped her wrists, holding them above her head, while he studied her flushed face.

'Now beg me to take you,' he said slowly, in a hard voice. 'Beg me, Storm, the way you begged me to spare David's feelings.'

Revulsion surged through her, her mind suddenly crystal clear, her body stiffening with rejection, as she tensed beneath him. Had she really forgotten all his threats? And the scene she had interrupted in the library only hours before? No wonder he found it so effortless to stem his passion—it was probably only simulated anyway, she decided on a wave of self-disgust, and her eyes darkened as she tried to pull free.

'Let me go!'

Her unsteady whisper brought a mocking smile to his lips. 'No way. We've reached the point of no return, Storm, and if you won't say it now, you will in the final moment of possession.'

His claim scorched her with shame, its arrogant certainty making her writhe helplessly as his body lowered on to hers, her flailing hands pinioned effortlessly against him as his mouth fastened on hers in hard demand, ignoring all attempts to break free. Desire shuddered through her, but she fought against it, her mind no longer blunted by passion.

The pressure of his thighs hurt, sending panic ricocheting through her as she struggled frenziedly to escape. His mouth burned where it touched, her body ice-cold with fear.

'Don't—please!'

She felt him stiffen, his voice incredulous and bitter. 'Skip the frightened virgin bit. David might go for it, but it turns me off.' When she didn't move his weight suddenly shifted, and light almost blinded her as he switched on a bedside lamp, his hands cupping her face, forcing it into the light as he studied her. 'The truth this time, Storm. Are you trying to tell me that you're a virgin?'

His voice had a flat metallic ring, and Storm closed her eyes, unable to bear the expression in his.

'You know I am,' she said bitterly. 'You've thrown it in my face often enough—telling me I'm not womanly, telling me . . .'

'That was when I . . . Oh, God!' he swore suddenly, rolling away from her and leaving her cold and numb. 'Open your eyes,' he commanded in a harsh voice, 'and for heaven's sake stop looking at me like that!'

He had pulled on his robe, his face oddly pale in the soft light. He disappeared and came back with her clothes, which he handed to her in grim silence.

'I don't make love with virgins,' he told her derisively. 'Get dressed, I'm taking you home. He burst out when she didn't move, 'You crazy little fool! Have you any idea...' He shook his head slowly, as though it pained him, and stared broodingly down at her. 'Of course you damned well don't,' he said bitterly at last. 'Well, I'm not David, Storm, I can't take you to my bed and act the heroic lily-white knight. For two pins I could damn you and your precious virginity to eternal hell. Have you any idea...' He stopped himself with visible effort, his muscles rigid beneath the thin silk robe as he scooped up the quilt and flung it over her. 'Get dressed,' he commanded again, and turned on his heel.

Just for a moment she had an insane desire to beg him to come back to her; to tell him there was no one she would rather have initiate her into becoming a woman, but the set of his shoulders killed the impulse as it was born, her voice shaky as she whispered, 'But you said...'

'I don't give a damn what I said, Storm,' he told her savagely. 'Get dressed—unless you're sure you can take the inevitable.'

His expression left her in no doubt that he meant what he said. When he had gone, she pulled on her clothes with hands that trembled and ten minutes later she was sitting silently at his side as he drove her home.

'I'm not going to apologise for what happened,' he told her harshly as he pulled up in front of the house. 'So for God's sake stop looking at me like that. No—no tears, please,' he swore as he saw the betraying glisten on her cheeks. 'You've still got your precious virginity—now get out before I take you back with me and really give you something to cry about!'

It seemed that she had spent the whole night getting dressed and undressed, Storm thought miserably as she crept into her own cold bed.

Of course she couldn't sleep; all she could think about

was how she had felt in Jago's arms and the unappeased ache deep down inside the pit of her stomach. If only he hadn't made that impossible demand, she thought wretchedly she might now have been sleeping in his arms. The thought caused fresh tears.

She drifted off to sleep towards dawn, and woke up to the rattle of tea cups. At first she thought she must still be at Jago's, but when she opened her eyes, she gave a gasp of startled surprise. 'Ian!'

'And where were you last night, you little vamp?' her brother teased with a grin, dropping down beside her when her smile crumbled and tears filled her eyes. 'Hey, come on! This isn't my tough, battling sister...'

'Is that how you see me?' she asked forlornly, taking the handkerchief he proffered. 'Am I really so unfeminine?'

'Want to tell me about it?' he invited. 'And don't say there's nothing to tell. When my kid sister comes home in the early hours of the morning and bursts into tears the moment I speak to her, it doesn't take a genius to work out what's happened. Who is he?' he teased. 'Anyone I know? Lord, it's not old David, is it?'

Storm shook her head.

'No, it's not David, but don't ask me any more, Ian. It's hopeless anyway. He doesn't give a damn about me. Tell me about you. Did you know that John's getting married?'

They caught up on each other's news over breakfast, which Ian insisted on preparing, his pyjama-clad body fit and muscular, his skin tanned from long exposure to the sun.

'I wanted to get back in time for your birthday,' he told her over a second cup of coffee, 'but owing to a hold-up at Heathrow I didn't quite make it. Just as well really, I never stopped to think that you might be out.'

'It was only a party down the road,' Storm told him

expressionlessly, 'you could have come with me. I'd better go and have a shower and get dressed.'

'Don't use all the hot water!' Ian called after her with a brotherly grin, reminiscent of their adolescence. 'And put on your best gear, I'm taking you out for lunch.'

It was a grey, miserable day, in keeping with her mood, and Storm lingered under the stinging spray of the shower, hoping that somehow the pain would drive out the agony inflicted by Jago.

'Bathroom's free, Ian,' she called downstairs as she padded into her bedroom. She didn't really feel like going out, but Ian would be disappointed if she refused.

As she walked into the kitchen the back door opened and Jago's broad shoulders were framed in the doorway.

'Storm, I've come to . . .' He broke off, staring at Ian who, dressed only in pyjama trousers, was reading the paper.

'Bathroom's free,'. Storm reminded her brother. He glanced from her to Jago and whistled tunelessly between his teeth, smacking Storm lightly on the rump with the folded paper as he shuffled past her.

'Don't forget our lunch date,' he told her lightly, and Storm's heart sank as she read the questions in his eyes. No doubt once Jago had gone and they were alone he would drag the truth out of her.

Jago's face was bone-white, temper blazing out of his eyes as he advanced on her.

'My God, you little bitch!' he said softly when Ian had gone. 'You damned near sent me crazy last night with that pitiful little tale about being a virgin, and I fell for it!' His hands gripped her shoulders and his fingers bit into the tender flesh. 'I spent the rest of the night telling myself I was a heel for doing what I did to you, and I came round this morning to make sure you were all right. All right! I don't need to use much imagination to know what you were doing! No wonder you were so anxious to

come home. Do your parents know about their lodger?'
The violence of his accusations caught Storm off guard.

'You don't understand,' she began, grasping when he
shook her.

'What do you take me for? Of course I understand.
I'll bet he's something Winters didn't know about. Who
is he? Some local Romeo who flits from bed to bed as the
fancy takes him?'

A slow burning anger rose inside her like a floodtide,
drowning out everything but its bitter strength.

'Yes, he spent the night here,' she cried defiantly. 'I'm
sorry if it offends your pride to think I've given someone
else what I wouldn't give you, but he gives me something
you never could. He loves me,' she said fiercely, watching
his eyes darken ominously, his anger only urging her
recklessly on. 'You wanted to use me, Jago,' she accused,
'so you can hardly complain if I used you. Now will you
please leave?' She turned her back on him, but he grabbed
hold of her, swinging her back against him, crushing her
mouth with the angry pressure of his kiss, forcing the soft
tender flesh back against her lips with passionate intensity.
His hands hurt as he forced her against him, grasping her
neck and holding it while his mouth continued its bitter
punishment. When he released her his eyes glittered like
jet, his breathing harsh as his eyes swept her contemptuously.

'You really had me fooled, but you're just like all the
rest, aren't you?'

When the door finally slammed behind him Storm
stumbled to a chair, her mind and body blessedly numb.

It was better like this, she told herself over and over
again; this way at least she retained a little of her pride,
and he would never know that while he tore her to shreds
with his angry words, inside she was slowly dying for love
of him.

She heard Ian whistling as he came downstairs and

quickly tried to force a smile. But when he looked at her she knew she hadn't deceived him.

'Storm! My God, what's he done to you?' His eyes went to the door. Storm restrained him instinctively, flushing at the blaze of anger in his face as he looked at her revealing mouth.

'He thought that you . . . he thought we were lovers,' she said helplessly. 'Last night . . .'

'He made love to you and thought you'd gone straight from his arms to mine, is that it?' Ian asked incredulously.

Storm shook her head, moistening her lips. 'He didn't make love to me in the sense that you mean, Ian. That's just it. But he thought that you and I . . .'

'Poor sod,' Ian said softly, his expression lightening as he looked into her shocked face. 'You really are an innocent, aren't you? By some miracle he manages to keep his hands off you, and what does he find when he turns up on your doorstep full of apologies and remorse? A strange male obviously very much at home and in a state of partial nudity.' Ian started to laugh, sobering abruptly when he saw Storm's face. 'I'm sorry. He's important to you, isn't he? Let me tell him . . .'

'No!' Storm clutched at his sleeve, her face paper-white. 'It wouldn't do any good, Ian, and besides, it's better like this.'

'I'm not having him think what he does about my sister,' Ian retorted stubbornly. 'And besides, he has a right to know the truth, Storm. What he thinks he saw will be eating into his guts like acid. Let me . . .'

'It's too late. He's just driven past,' Storm told him as she saw the familiar green car sweep past the end of the drive. 'Just leave it, Ian. It's over.'

She didn't really feel like going out for lunch, but she went for her brother's sake. He took her to a small country pub where they ate their meal in relaxed surroundings, and afterwards Ian went up to the bar to get them both a drink.

'Hello there!'

Storm turned at the familiar voice, smiling at Greg Harmer. When Ian returned she introduced them as Greg explained that he was with his father, who as a widower preferred to lunch out.

'He still misses my mother very badly,' Greg told them, 'and I've often wished he would remarry. If you've finished eating why don't you join us for a drink? I know he'd like to see you again, Storm.'

'After all that's happened with his advertising.' Storm asked a little bitterly, quickly explaining to Ian.

He raised his eyebrows and frowned. 'Typical of David Winters,' he said angrily. 'I never did like him.'

Ian and Greg seemed to have hit it off quite well, and knowing that her brother sometimes found his long leaves hanging heavily on his hands now that his old friends had left the Cotswolds, Storm welcomed the chance meeting.

Mr Harmer couldn't have been more charming, keeping her well entertained while Greg and Ian exchanged university reminiscences. There was only a year between them, and Greg questioned Ian eagerly about his experiences abroad.

Listening to her brother, Storm felt a small glow of pride. The responsibilities his job entailed had given him an air of authority, and trying to observe him through a stranger's eyes she could see that he was a man who commanded respect and attention.

'Look,' Greg said a little awkwardly as they got up to leave, 'don't think I'm being pushy, but how about making up a foursome one evening? My sister Julia is a schoolteacher, but she's between jobs at the moment. She's got the wanderlust bug like you,' he said to Ian with a grin. 'She was working in Spain for a while teaching English, and now she's been offered a job in Saudi Arabia doing some private tuition. She would have been with us today, but she only got back late last night, so we left her in bed.'

'I'm sure Ian doesn't want to have Julia foisted off on him,' Mr Harmer started to protest, but Ian laughed, and accepted the invitation, after a querying smile at Storm.

It was arranged that Greg would pick them up the following evening, and as they drove home Ian told Storm that he was quite looking forward to it.

'Greg Harmer quite fancies you,' he told her with a sideways glance, and Storm responded with a brief smile. She knew quite well that with the slightest encouragement Greg would step into the empty space left by David, but she had learned her lesson now, and knew that it was pointless to get involved in another tepid relationship—pointless and unfair to Greg.

Storm had several days' holiday due to her, and when Ian said that he had a month's leave she decided that she might as well take them and spend as much time with him as she could.

There was no sign of Jago when she went to work on Monday morning. Ian drove her so that he could have the use of Mr Templeton's car during the day, and after reminding her of their date that evening, told her that he intended to have a lazy day getting accustomed to the cold English climate.

'I thought your parents were away,' Pete commented when Storm walked into the reception office. His sharp eyes didn't miss much, she reflected, shrugging off her coat.

'Ian's home,' she told him. 'He brought me to work. Any progress with the foster-parent appeal?'

Accepting the change of subject, Pete gestured enthusiastically to the large pile of mail on the desk.

'An even better response than I'd expected. I'm going over to the home this morning to chat to some of the kids, see how they'll come over on interview. Want to come with me?'

Mary Simmonds greeted them enthusiastically, offering them coffee and biscuits as they sat down in her shabby study.

'I can't tell you how delighted we are with what you're doing. We've already placed several of the smaller children,' she explained to Storm. 'Not on a permanent basis, of course. These things can't be rushed. But several couples have come forward offering to act as "aunts and uncles". Most of them have grown-up children of their own and are aware of the hazards and pitfalls.'

'And the children?' Storm asked.

'Oh, they're loving it. We're being very careful not to let them get too excited before anything actually happens, but it's going to make such a difference in their lives, even if it's only the odd outing and visit. To children like these just to have someone pay them individual attention means so very, very much.'

'The older kids are going to be more of a problem,' Pete said frankly. 'Teenagers are difficult at the best of times.'

'You're quite right,' Mary Simmonds sighed. 'And these children more than most are suffering from such a sense of rejection that it makes them automatically withdraw into themselves; sometimes even deliberately scorning the thing they want most. You see, they've been without individual love and attention for so long that they've convinced themselves that they don't really want it. I was wondering if Mr Marsh might come and talk to some of them,' she said quietly to Storm. 'His success might encourage them and provide the spur we need.'

Not sure if Pete was aware of Jago's background, Storm said hurriedly that she was having a few days' holiday but that Pete would mention the matter to him.

When the cups had been cleared away, several gangly

teenagers were brought into the room, and introduced to them. They were awkward, and inclined to eye them warily, and Storm's heart went out to them. Pete had exactly the right touch, she acknowledged, listening to him drawing them out as he asked about their interests. 'How about coming on my show?' he asked when they had eventually relaxed.

'So that everyone can feel sorry for us?' one tall, thin boy muttered suspiciously. He was about fifteen with a shock of brown hair and wary, defensive eyes, and Storm found herself holding her breath as she waited to see how Pete would handle him.

'Do you think they ought to?' Pete asked casually. 'I reckon most teenagers would envy you, eh, Storm? No parents moaning about loud music and untidy bedrooms.' When the laughter had died down Pete said seriously, 'Look, no one wants to force any of you into something you don't want. How you feel about becoming a member of a family is something personal and very private—no one denies that. But wanting to be part of a family is nothing to be ashamed of, you know. And it isn't all one-sided. There's lots of folk out there whose kids have left home, or perhaps who never had any, who would give their right arm for the chance of fostering . . .'

'Yeah, as long as it's a kid under five,' another of the boys jeered resentfully. 'When it comes to us, no one wants to know.'

'That's where I think you're wrong,' Pete said quietly. 'But the choice is yours and I don't want you to make it right now. Think about it, and then next week I'll be along to talk to you again. Even if you don't want to be on my show, you can still come and have a look round the studios. The invitation doesn't come from me, it's from Mr Marsh,' he told them as he stood up. 'So think about it, okay?'

'I think you managed to get through to them,' Mary

Simmonds announced when the children had gone.

Pete looked embarrassed. 'Oh, Jago suggested that might be the best way to approach them. He seems to have a pretty good idea how their minds work.'

'Yes, he does,' Mary Simmonds agreed, smiling at Storm. 'I'll look forward to seeing you next week, then.'

It was no good letting pity for the boy Jago had been overwhelm her, Storm decided on the way back to the studios. He wasn't that boy any longer. He was a man, hardened by his experiences, and any attempt on her part to breach his cynical exterior would only result in more pain—for her.

CHAPTER TEN

IT was obvious that no matter what her feelings might be, Ian was enjoying himself, Storm admitted as she looked at her brother's animated face.

To her dismay Greg Harmer had booked them a table at the Country Club, and Storm had found it virtually impossible to touch her food, remembering the lunch she had had here with Jago and its aftermath.

Julia Harmer had turned out to be a vivacious redhead, with a warm smile and sparkling blue eyes, and Storm suspected that under his quizzical teasing Ian was completely bowled over. He was certainly being far more attentive than mere politeness demanded, and Storm suspected that he was already regretting their foursome. A simple twosome would be much more to his taste, judging by the looks he was giving Julia.

'Something worrying you?' Greg asked when she had neglected to answer him for the third time. 'You seem a bit preoccupied.'

'It's nothing,' Storm assured him. 'I'm sorry, I'm spoiling your evening.'

'Forget it,' he told her gallantly. 'Shall we dance?'

Julia and Ian were already on the floor, unashamedly making the most of the slow seductive music. Storm was glad when Greg made no attempt to hold her intimately, and her breath came in a shocked gasp as she felt someone looking at her and turned her head to see Jago and Madeleine Rivers sitting at a table next to the dance floor.

'Do you mind if we sit down?' she asked Greg in a shaky voice. She doubted if her legs would continue to hold her much longer, they felt so weak and trembly.

'Sure. Do you want me to get your brother?' Greg asked solicitously, obviously concerned by her pale face and compressed lips.

Ian was still dancing with Julia, her head curved against his shoulder, and Storm had no wish to spoil his evening.

'It's nothing,' she told Greg. 'But it's been a long day. Would you mind if I went home? I can get a taxi...'

'You'll do no such thing,' Greg told her firmly. 'And besides, something tells me that neither Julia nor Ian will really mind us deserting them. I'll leave them a note and then we can go.'

Storm went to get her coat, grateful for his unquestioning understanding. On her way to the cloakroom, she scrupulously avoided looking in the direction of Jago's table, the breath almost knocked out of her body when hard hands suddenly grasped her waist, almost pulling her off balance.

'Jago!' She stared up at him, her face white and her eyes strained.

'Jago!' he mimicked savagely. 'What are you playing at? Turn and turn about—is that the way it goes?' The ugliness of his voice made her feel acutely sick. 'I suppose you've got to find some means of enlivening the long winter nights, but I never suspected you went in for orgies. Can anyone join in, or do you have to pass some sort of endurance test first?'

Madeleine emerged from the cloakroom, her eyes glittering coldly over Storm as Jago released her.

'Honestly, darling I don't know why you brought me here,' she complained, linking her arm through Jago's. 'You know I would much rather be alone with you.' The blatant invitation made Storm feel ill. She stumbled past them, not caring what Jago might read in her eyes, if he was ever able to remove them from his companion.

When she and Greg got outside it was raining. There

was no sign of the Ferrari in the car-park, and Storm
tried not to picture Jago's lean body embracing Madeleine.

Much to her relief Greg made no attempt to kiss her
goodnight. She didn't think she could have borne even
the lightest embrace. Much to her surprise, when she went
to bed she fell asleep almost straight away, waking
momentarily when a car door slamming told her that Ian
had returned.

'You okay?' he called softly outside her door, coming in
when she murmured a reply.

'Did you get a taxi?' she asked him sleepily, but he
shook his head.

'Nope, we managed to get a lift. Your friend Jago
Marsh.' Storm's heart missed a beat, but before she could
question him further, Ian had gone. So Jago had not left
with Madeleine as she had thought, but what did it matter
when he left, she asked herself sleepily, the result would
be the same. Madeleine had made it pretty clear how she
expected to finish the evening.

Storm woke up early, struggling through layers of sleep to
the realisation that she could not continue in this fashion.
Her acute awareness of Jago was making it impossible for
her to function properly, and would soon begin to affect
her performance at work. She would have to persuade
him to release her from her contract—which shouldn't be
too difficult, she admitted numbly. By now he must be as
anxious to get rid of her as she was to leave.

It was a cold raw morning, with the sky threatening
rain or even snow, and Storm shivered as she ate her
breakfast. She took Ian a cup of tea, which he drank
sleepily, before telling her that he had promised to take
Julia out for lunch.

'You can come with us, if you like,' he offered, but
Storm shook her head.

'And play gooseberry?' she teased, laughing at the colour mounting in his face.

Back downstairs a restlessness drove her and on impulse she pulled on an old anorak, scribbling Ian a note on the message pad her mother kept in the kitchen. Perhaps a walk would help to clear her brain, and at least the activity would give her something to do other than brood.

Storm knew the countryside round her home like the back of her hand, and let her feet take her automatically along the narrow sheep trails lacing the hills behind the house.

The old ruined monastery nestling next to the river which ran through the village was a favourite childhood haunt, and the remnants of the once proud walls offered some protection from the biting wind. Her anorak wasn't really warm enough for this weather, Storm acknowledged as she huddled in the lee of the building watching some birds searching for food.

As a child she had rebuilt the monastery in her imagination, pretending it was still the bustling community it had once been, trying to picture the lives of the monks who had lived here. They would have been a rich, happy band, for in the Middle Ages the wool from Cotswold sheep had been worth its weight in gold and this monastery had owned many rich acres. But with the Dissolution had come poverty, the community disbanded and the monks left to roam and scavenge a living where they could.

Stiff and cold, Storm got to her feet. She had walked farther than she intended and already it seemed to be getting dark. The winter afternoons were so short, and as she started to walk back needle-sharp flurries of rain were driving against her body, soaking through her thin jacket within minutes.

On her outward journey Storm had barely noticed the steep climb to the monastery, but going back the rain made the narrow path treacherous, and several times she slipped in the mud, acknowledging that her shoes were not really suitable for serious walking.

She was shivering and cold, her hair plastered to her skull by the driving rain. She tried to walk faster, conscious that Ian must be wondering where she was. She hadn't realised how long she had been sitting dreaming of the past.

A bird flew out of the undergrowth in front of her, startling her, and she slipped in the mud, her hands going out to break her fall. The impact of the hard ground knocked the breath from her body, and she lay there for several seconds trying to find the strength to get to her feet. As she sat up a sharp pain lanced through her right ankle. Shivering with cold, she tried to move her foot. The pain was excruciating, but she was able to do so, so at least she hadn't broken the bone, she told herself thankfully, but there was no way she was going to be able to walk the two or three miles home.

Biting hard on her lip, she managed to drag herself a few yards, but it was hopelessly slow progress, draining every ounce of energy. She tried to stand up, wondering if she could limp slowly down the path, but after a few paces she knew that there was no way she could make it. She tried to remember how far it was to the nearest house. She was too far down the hills to be near a farm, and with a feeling of hopeless despair she acknowledged that she could do nothing but wait for someone to find her. Fighting down her hysteria, she refused to dwell on how long that might be. Ian knew she had gone for a walk, but he had no idea where. Even if he had already raised the alert it would be hours before anyone found her. Cursing herself for being so stupid, Storm willed herself to keep calm. It would only be a matter of time before she was found; all she had to do was to try and keep warm and as dry as possible. She managed to crawl to an outcrop of rocks which provided some shelter from the wind and rain, but her teeth were chattering fiercely by the time she had done so, and she acknowledged that if the temperature dropped much further she had scant chance of retaining much body heat.

After what seemed like an eternity a hazy sleepiness started to engulf her, and although she knew she ought to fight against it, it seemed much easier and pleasanter to give in and close her eyes. She slept, tormented by images of Jago, some so real that she cried out despairingly, begging him to leave her in peace. At one point she even thought she heard his voice calling her name, and she croaked an instinctive response.

Someone was shaking her roughly, rubbing her arms and legs until needle-sharp pains lanced through them. She tried to escape the briskly impersonal hands, but they would not set her free.

'Open your, eyes Storm,' someone commanded.

It was too much of an effort to disobey. Storm opened them reluctantly, and looked straight into the icy grey depths of Jago's. She shivered violently and was pulled against him, something warm and soft sliding over her cold body. She fingered it absently, smothering hysteria. Wool! It was something woolly off the sheep whose paths had led to her downfall!

She started to laugh helplessly, shocked into abrupt silence as Jago hit her with his open palm.

'No hysterics,' he told her curtly. 'What happened?'

The sharp stinging pain brought her back to reality. 'I fell,' she told him, 'and I think I've sprained my ankle, but how . . .'

'No questions now,' he told her, swinging her up against him. 'Lie still.'

It seemed easier to give in than to argue, and besides, her mind was too tired to battle with the problem of how Jago of all people had found her on this isolated path. His heart beneath her cheek made a soothing sound and she felt herself relaxing into his warmth.

'Wake up, Storm,' he told her roughly, shaking her, and she thought she heard him add, 'I'm not going to lose you now,' but she knew that she must be mistaken.

It was a relief to see the welcoming lights ahead of them, and she made no demur when a door opened and warmth seeped through her. She was lying on something and it was far too much effort to open her eyes again. She could hear Jago moving about and caught the faint, distant 'ping' as he lifted a telephone receiver. Odd words impinged upon her consciousness, but without form or meaning, and then Jago was back, squatting on his haunches at her side, forcing her to open her eyes and listen to him.

'I've rung the doctor, and your brother. The doctor's going to come round later and check you over, but I don't think you've broken anything.' His eyes narrowed as Storm shivered convulsively. 'We've got to get you out of those wet clothes . . .'

'Ian . . .' Storm murmured, wanting him to take her home, but her plea was ignored as Jago lifted her in his arms, the sleeves of the sweater he had wrapped round her covering her hands.

'Keep still,' he told her roughly as she twisted in his arms.

Despite her cold, despite everything, the moment he touched her a yearning ache sprang to life. Her hands linked behind his neck, an overwhelming urge rising inside her to bury them in the thick darkness of his hair. She trembled suddenly, her aching ankle forgotten, wondering at the sudden compression of Jago's mouth as he felt her involuntary response.

He didn't take her to the blue and grey bedroom and for that she was thankful, until she realised that the bed he was placing her on was his own, the cream and brown decor undeniably masculine, his leather jacket thrown carelessly over a chair.

'If I hadn't found you when I did, do you realise what would have happened to you?' he asked mercilessly, watching her. 'When Ian came over here and told me what you'd done I could barely credit it.'

'Ian came here?' Her attention was riveted on him, despite the terrible cold in her body. She licked her lips warily.

'You little fool!' he said roughly. 'Why the hell didn't you tell me he was your brother instead of letting me think . . .' He broke off as she turned away to hide the weak tears filling her eyes. 'Get those wet clothes off. There's a bathroom through there,' he told her nodding towards a closed door. 'You'll have to make do with one of my sweaters until Ian gets here with your clothes.'

'You should have taken me straight home,' Storm protested, but he ignored her, and strode to the door, where he turned to eye her critically. 'There wouldn't have been much point. Ian's over at Harmers. He came over to see me before he went to pick up Julia. He told me you'd gone out—I wouldn't have been in myself, but I'd been to London and wanted to collect some papers I left here. When it got dark and there were no signs of life from your place I rang Ian at Harmers to find out if he had any idea where you might have gone.' His voice was exceedingly grim. 'He told me that particular path used to be one of your favourites. It's lucky for you he's got such a good memory.'

Storm wasn't listening. A terrible cold had invaded her body. As she struggled to remove his sweater, her fingers refused to obey her, and fumbled clumsily with the welt. She tried to sit up, smothering a cry as she jarred her ankle.

Jago was beside her immediately.

'Don't touch me!' she cried bitterly, shrinking away

from him, terrified that her body would betray her to him. Even feeling as she did at the moment, she was still nerve-shatteringly aware of him.

His face closed up, his eyes hard and cold. 'Don't be a fool,' he told her abruptly. 'You've nothing to fear from me now, Storm. Now let me help you. Don't you know how near you are to hypothermia?' he asked bleakly when she continued to shrink away.

When she didn't answer, he leaned forward, grasping her shoulders and pulling the sweater over her head, before turning back to unzip her anorak. It was soaked right through, the thin blouse she was wearing underneath plastered to her skin. She froze as Jago started to unfasten the buttons, but she needn't have worried, his touch was totally impersonal.

What had he meant when he said she had nothing to fear from him now? Had the fact that she was still a virgin turned him off completely? Did he no longer even want her? She couldn't stop the dismay the thought brought, and went limp in his arms as he removed her blouse. She heard him curse as her teeth chattered betrayingly, and as a terrible tiredness reached out to claim her she saw him disappear in the direction of the bathroom.

When he came back he shook her roughly. In the distance she could hear the sound of water, and for a moment she thought she was still lying outside in the rain.

'I'm so cold,' she complained wretchedly, shivering under his hands.

She thought he said something, but she didn't catch it, and his voice was so grim she thought it was probably just as well.

As he tugged off her wet jeans she was too exhausted to protest, moaning softly as he touched her ankle. Dimly she was aware of him removing her briefs and bra, then he was picking her up—taking her where? she wondered stupidly, struggling feebly in his arms.

At first when she felt the stinging spray of the shower, she didn't realise what was happening. The water was deliciously warm and she sighed softly, her body limp as she gave herself up to the reviving heat. She wanted to lie down, to bask in the comforting warmth, to close her eyes and sleep for ever on a hot sandy beach with the sun pouring its heat over her body.

'Stand up!' Jago commanded her tersely, and her eyes flew open, the hazy dream dispelled, as she realised what was happening. Jago's shirt was plastered to his body, his jeans soaking wet as he held her under the spray.

'Let me go,' she mumbled, trying to stand. Pain shot through her ankle and she sobbed out loud, her fists pounding the dampness of his chest.

'Leave me alone . . . I hate you . . . I hate you!'

'If I leave you now, you'll probably drown,' his cool voice jeered. 'Now be a good girl and let's get you warm and dry. Think of it as nasty but necessary medicine,' he drawled, 'and when it's all over, we'll get you tucked up safely with your teddy bear and some warm milk.'

'I don't have a teddy bear,' Storm protested hazily.

'No? Well, you certainly aren't up to the only other thing you can cuddle up to to keep warm, are you?'

The derisive words stung. She tried to push him away, but was far too weak. Despite the warmth of the water, she was still cold, with a deep inner coldness that warned her of the truth of Jago's assertion that she had been close to succumbing to hypothermia.

She shivered again, and this time wasn't given the chance to protest as he forced her back under the shower, its spray hotter this time, her body suddenly moltenly alive with sensation as Jago reached behind her squirting some tangy, masculine body shampoo into his hand and massaging it into her skin.

'Not precisely what the doctor ordered,' he said dryly,

'but it's one way of getting your circulation back to normal.'

'I thought brandy was the time-honoured method,' Storm managed to mutter through chattering teeth, but Jago shook his head, his mouth compressing.

'Not for hypothermia; the one thing you mustn't do is fall asleep, and that's exactly what you would have done if I'd given you brandy . . .'

'I can manage myself,' she protested thickly as his hand touched her thigh. All at once heat flooded through her, her body suddenly surging to life beneath his hands, her trembling no longer caused by cold but by a desire so intense she could barely contain it. Smothering a groan, she pulled away from him, caught off balance as he jerked her back, clamping her against him.

With a fevered moan she arched convulsively against him, his name on her lips as she thrust her hands into the thick darkness of his hair, her mouth opening eagerly beneath his, the feel of his body against her intensely pleasurable. Nothing existed except the way he was making her feel. With small moans of pleasure she kissed the hard warmth of his throat, his hoarse protest only inciting her to strain closer to him, her fingers impatient with his shirt buttons. In the end he helped her, tugging his shirt off and supporting them both against the tiled wall of the shower as her hands moved feverishly over his chest, her lips nuzzling his throat as his mouth caressed her shoulders.

Beneath her touch the feel of his dampened skin excited her. Her hands dropped to his waist and as though reading her thoughts, Jago muttered harshly, 'God, Storm, don't make me do this,' but she was beyond caution or reason. Her fingers fumbled with his belt, and with a groan Jago pushed her away.

'Please . . .' she begged huskily, her eyes dark with passion, and swayed towards him.

'Oh Storm, don't you know what you're doing to me?' Jago protested hoarsely, removing the offending jeans.

With a sigh of blissful contentment Storm melted against him, revelling in the way he shuddered against her as she slid her arms round his neck and pulled his head down.

Even if he didn't love her, he wanted her, and no power on earth could take that from her.

She closed her eyes and stretched sensuously against him, her heart pounding as she felt him move against her. Her hands slid down over his shoulders, following the line of dark hair to the flatness of his stomach, then her wanton downward exploration was stopped forcibly.

'For God's sake, Storm,' Jago muttered feverishly, holding her off, 'what are you trying to do to me?'

His eyes were smoky with desire, his face faintly flushed, and he was breathing as though he had been running— hard.

'Only what you're doing to me,' Storm admitted, abandoning the last of her self-restraint and pressing herself against him. Keeping her eyes on his face, she whispered against his mouth, 'Take me, Jago. I want you so badly. Please!' she begged feverishly, when he made no response, tears of frustration glittering in her eyes. 'Please love me, Jago,' she pleaded, brushing her lips against his throat.

His body shuddered against her, his mouth claiming hers in a kiss of intense need, fuelling a fire that left her pliant and trembling, an ache in her body telling her there could be only one satisfactory outcome.

When the kiss ended she opened her eyes in mute appeal. 'Don't stop,' she whispered achingly. 'I want you so much. I love you so much,' she whispered frenziedly. 'But you knew that all the time, didn't you? And now that I've admitted it the game's over, isn't it? You don't want me any more . . .'

All at once he thrust her away, tears filling her eyes at the roughness of his hands on her shoulders.

'Say that again!' he breathed urgently.

'You don't want me any more . . .'

'Not that,' he groaned, trembling. 'Tell me you love me again. God, if you knew what I've been through waiting to hear you say that . . . So many times I thought you would, but always you pulled back, throwing Winters in my face. Are you telling the truth?' he muttered unevenly, his eyes searching her face.

'I wouldn't admit to myself that what I felt for you was more than desire,' Storm told him bravely. 'I never wanted to feel like this about anyone.' Her eyes dropped. 'I've always been frightened that some day I would, and that it would be like handing over a part of myself to someone for all time . . .'

'And is it?' Jago asked softly, his thumbs caressing the fragile bones of her jaw.

'Worse,' Storm admitted with a wry smile. 'I can't fight you any longer, Jago. I'm yours for as long as you want me, even if it means sharing you with the Madeleines of this world . . . Don't you want me now?' she cried bitterly when he made no move to take her back in his arms. 'Is that it? Now that I've capitulated and you've got what you wanted . . .'

He swung her round suddenly, fierce passion in his eyes.

'I'll never have enough of you, Storm. There isn't that much time; not even in a thousand lifetimes.'

He picked her up, pulling a thick fleecy towel from the rail and wrapping her in it before depositing her on the bed, while he shrugged on a towelling robe.

'Now,' he said softly, bending to take her in his arms, 'with that delectable body covered up, I might recover enough of my self-control to talk to you. Don't look at me like that,' he added roughly. 'If you know how much I've wanted you here like this! The other night, when you looked at me and told me you were a virgin, I could willingly have killed you.' He groaned at the memory. 'I wanted you so badly, and I told myself that it didn't matter that you didn't love me. I turned you on, and I thought I could teach you to care, in time, but when I knew that I would be the first, that you hadn't had any other lovers, I knew I couldn't take from you what should only be given in love. I didn't get much sleep that night, I can tell you. And then in the morning, when I came to tell you that I loved you, and that I wanted to start again, and I saw Ian sitting there half naked, I felt as though I was being eaten alive with jealousy.'

'Is that why you were so angry?'

'Angry? I damn near burst a blood vessel! When I thought of you with him . . . I didn't know what I wanted most—to strangle you with my bare hands, or to hear you crying my name in that little soft voice you only use when we're making love. I love you, Storm,' he said abruptly, searching her face. 'More than I can ever tell you. Will you marry me?'

Happiness flooded through her, her body trembling with eagerness as she reached up towards him.

His kisses had a new tenderness, his expression was rueful as he pulled the towel firmly round her.

'Having waited this long, I can wait a little longer, but not too long,' he warned her huskily. 'The moment your parents get back we're getting married. I guess they'll want the full works, white dress and all, but no more scenes like this. My self-control is a mite precarious. You do things to me that I didn't think possible.'

'What about Madeleine?' Storm asked jealously, her eyes darkening as she remembered the pain she had experienced when she saw him with the other girl.

'Madeleine's a girl who doesn't understand the meaning of the word no,' Jago told her dryly. 'What you thought you saw in my study was her way of trying to convince me that I should help her with her career. If you hadn't run off when you did, you'd have seen me telling her that I haven't reached the stage yet where I need to pay for my sex.'

'I think I've loved you right from the beginning,' Storm confessed, 'But I was so frightened I clung to David, knowing that my independence would never be threatened by him. Every time you touched me I wanted you more, but I kept telling myself it was just desire . . .'

'You were driving me mad,' Jago admitted. 'I knew I was getting through to you physically, although you wouldn't admit it, but that wasn't enough. Every time you told me you loved Winters I had to stop myself from forcibly tearing him apart. You've put me through hell these last few weeks,' he whispered huskily, kissing her deeply, 'but soon I'll be in heaven.'

Storm melted against him, knowing there was no longer any need to pretend, her response instinctive and total.

When Jago raised his head, he was breathing heavily, his taut muscles betraying the self-control he was exerting.

'When did you know that you loved me?' Storm murmured, her hands stroking his skin. He captured them, smiling wryly.

'Do you want an imbecile for a husband? If so you're going the right way to drive me completely out of my mind. If you must have the truth,' he said softly, 'I fell head over heels in love with you the first time I saw you.'

'In David's office?'

He shook his head, his eyes gleaming.

'Long before that. The I.B.A. told me months ago that they were worried about Radio Wyechester. They take a keen interest in new stations—after all, they've got their reputation to consider and a bad station reflects badly on them. They asked me if I'd be interested in taking over because they knew that I was looking for something new. At first I refused. I remembered Winters from the B.B.C. I hadn't liked him then, and I didn't want to get involved with him again. Just out of idle curiosity I went through all the personal files the I.B.A. sent me. Yours was the first. The moment I opened it and saw your photograph, I knew that I was going to take over the station no matter what I had to do to get it. I was plotting your downfall long before you even knew it.

'Ian will be here soon with your clothes,' he added, 'and while I'm pretty sure he's in no doubt about the way I feel about you, I don't think he should find us like this. I got quite a shock when he introduced himself as your brother. When I saw you at the Country Club last night I could willingly have murdered you! What's the matter?' he asked as Storm placed her fingers against his lips.

'If Ian's going to come and interrupt us, I don't think we should waste time talking,' she said huskily, drawing him down against her, her mouth parting in mute invitation.

'Storm!' Jago groaned protestingly, but his hands were already sliding beneath the towel, sending explosive waves of delight coursing through her, his heart thudding betrayingly against her as he told her throatily of his love.

Harlequin Plus

THE EVOCATIVE COTSWOLDS

The setting of *Tiger Man,* by British author Penny Jordan, is the Cotswolds, a picturesque region of green, gently undulating hills only an hour or two by car from London. Yet despite its proximity to this international capital, the Cotswold area remains primarily well-groomed farmland remarkably unspoiled by urban sprawl.

Dotted here and there on a landscape where sheep graze peacefully are old stone villages almost untouched by time. Owner-occupied centuries-old houses and thriving eighteenth-century inns with cobblestone courtyards are both part of the historic charm and cannot help but evoke thoughts of romance and adventure of bygone days.

Even the names of the region's villages are romantic-sounding: Stowe-on-the-Wold, Bourton-on-the-Water, Chipping-Campden. One has the unlikely name of Broadway, perhaps because its main street is unusually wide. Broadway's old inns, tea shops and gift shops make it a great favorite with visitors.

In the summer, the Cotswolds' narrow country roads are crowded with cyclists, cars and sightseeing buses, but it's still possible to slip away to a secluded spot and enjoy the tranquillity, the soft breezes and the birdsong of this beautiful open countryside.

Readers all over the country say Harlequin is the best!

"You're #1."

A.H.*, Hattiesburg, Missouri

"Harlequin is the best in romantic reading."

K.G., Philadelphia, Pennsylvania

"I find Harlequins are the only stories on the market that give me a satisfying romance, with sufficient depth without being maudlin."

C.S., Bangor, Maine

"Keep them coming! They are still the best books."

R.W., Jersey City, New Jersey

*Names available on request.

Harlequin Presents...

Take these
4 best-selling novels
FREE

That's right! FOUR first-rate Harlequin romance novels by four world renowned authors, FREE, as your introduction to the Harlequin Presents Subscription Plan. Be swept along by these FOUR exciting, poignant and sophisticated novels . . . . Travel to the Mediterranean island of Cyprus in *Anne Hampson*'s "Gates of Steel" . . . to Portugal for *Anne Mather*'s "Sweet Revenge" . . . to France and *Violet Winspear*'s "Devil in a Silver Room" . . . and the sprawling state of Texas for *Janet Dailey*'s "No Quarter Asked."

Join the millions of avid Harlequin readers all over the world who delight in the magic of a really exciting novel. SIX great NEW titles published EACH MONTH! Each month you will get to know exciting, interesting, true-to-life people . . . . You'll be swept to distant lands you've dreamed of visiting . . . . Intrigue, adventure, romance, and the destiny of many lives will thrill you through each Harlequin Presents novel.

Harlequin Presents...

The very finest in romantic fiction

FREE Gift Certificate
and subscription reservation

Mail this coupon today!

In the U.S.A.
1440 South Priest Drive
Tempe, AZ 85281

In Canada
649 Ontario Street
Stratford, Ontario N5A 6W2

Harlequin Reader Service:

Please send me my 4 Harlequin Presents books free. Also, reserve a subscription to the 6 new Harlequin Presents novels published each month. Each month I will receive 6 new Presents novels at the low price of $1.75 each [*Total – $10.50 a month*]. There are no shipping and handling or any other hidden charges. I am free to cancel at any time, but even if I do, these first 4 books are still mine to keep absolutely FREE without any obligation.

NAME	(PLEASE PRINT)

ADDRESS

CITY	STATE / PROV.	ZIP / POSTAL CODE

Offer expires July 31, 1982   SB477
Offer not valid to present subscribers

Prices subject to change without notice.